THE WARREN COUNTY KILLINGS

Tom Strickland was a lawman – his elder brother Jack was an outlaw. After his release from jail, Jack and his woman disappeared and an accusation connected with his name put him once again on the wrong side of the law.

Meanwhile in Redrock, Tom came under suspicion and concluded that there was a conspiracy to remove him as Warren County sheriff. This belief proved well founded when it was rumoured that Jack was on the move. Violence became inevitable as Tom struggled to clear his name.

THE
WARREN COUNTY
KILLINGS

by

Frank Scarman

Dales Large Print Books
Long Preston, North Yorkshire,
BD23 4ND, England.

British Library Cataloguing in Publication Data.

Scarman, Frank
The Warren County killings.

A catalogue record of this book is
available from the British Library

ISBN   1-84262-015-0 pbk

First published in Great Britain by Robert Hale Limited, 1999

Published in Large Print 2000 by arrangement with
Robert Hale Limited

Dales Large Print is an imprint of Library Magna Books Ltd.

Printed and bound in Great Britain by
T.J. (International) Ltd., Cornwall, PL28 8RW

One

Like a dozen ants hastening over a smooth hummock of earth the posse out of Redrock was sticking to the task, and those whom it was seeking knew it, and reckoned that it was about time to abandon the bunch of horses they had been chivvying along and get themselves the hell and gone from there. And if one of their own mounts had not at that moment of decision suddenly gone lame, they might well have got clear.

Heading the posse, quirting strongly now that the quarry was in sight, the Warren County sheriff, Tom Strickland, had eleven men at his back. Two of them were his deputies, Nate Miller, along with five of his Rocking M hands; Jasper Fox, Jake Besant and Tex Faulkner. These last three Strickland could well have done without, but they had fronted up outside the county office as soon as word had gone out that a posse was wanted. And at the time, needing to be in saddles and away, Strickland could think of no reason for shutting them out; but he had no time at all for men of their stripe. True, he had had his problems with them in the past, once arresting Besant for drunkenness and firing off a pistol in the main street of Redrock; and there had been a couple of scuffles between them and his deputies in one of the rougher saloons, following disputes over cards. Strickland was thus very much aware that Besant and Faulkner regarded him with dislike and would take any opportunity that offered to see him discredited. The combination of these two with Jasper Fox was an unappealing one. A more intelligent man, Fox, and a manipulator.

But when the time came, when the posse finally came up with those who, according to Nate Miller, had got off with about ten of his saddle horses, it would be the rancher himself who could prove to be the real problem in this group. Miller was the chief reason that Strickland had decided to fetch along both of the county deputies, this against his normal inclinations.

The posse came thundering down a slope that was thickly covered in bunch-grass and sagebrush, then, swinging across to the right, went hauling around an outcrop of reddish rock, coming close to the mouth of a long, shallow valley of the Tessora Hills, and it was there, beyond a stand of tall, spindly, ghost-trunked aspens, that they caught sight of movement.

Miller yelled, 'There's the bastards! There they be!'

But what they had glimpsed turned out not to be the riders they sought but some horses running loose, Miller's horses, seen between the long trunks of the aspens, flickering across the line of sight at right angles. Even as the posse came spurring around the fringes of the tall trees, Miller was bawling for his riders to get out after the horses, get them rounded up, for indeed they were running free, though still tending to bunch together; and for the moment, no further sign of the men who had been with them. Not immediately. Until the pockmarked man, Faulkner, yelled, 'There!'

And indeed there they were, beginning to head up the long, wide valley. One of them, however, was having trouble, his horse apparently in some distress. The rider dismounted, hauling a rifle out of a scabbard, while the horse, stumbling, fell. Unhesitatingly the man shot it, then forted up behind the fallen animal, his still-mounted companion looking, weighing the situation before loping back to join the man on the ground, and swing down himself. His horse went trotting away, then stopped, its head turned towards the dismounted men.

Strickland called for his posse, now lacking the five Rocking M riders who had gone angling away towards the free-running horses, to haul up and not go riding in on top of men who were armed with rifles. So he and Miller, Fox and the two deputies, together with Faulkner and Besant, all came to a milling halt, horses blowing and tossing heads and side-stepping, their bit-chains clinking. A rifle lashed, the sound echoing up the valley. The bullet went breathing across the bunch of them, Strickland urgently waving his men back towards the cover of the aspens.

'Time's on our side. There's but two of 'em an' they're not going anywhere any more.'

Back in among the trees the possemen dismounted, unscabbarding their rifles. Both of Strickland's deputies returned on foot through the trees to keep an eye on what was happening. More shooting was heard from those in the valley, but presumably this was directed at the ranch riders who were still out in the open, after the horses.

Nate Miller, his jowly face deeply flushed let go a string of obscenities when he heard it.

'Go on, yuh bastards, shoot! Yuh ain't got much time left!'

Faulkner said, 'It's them Doyles, right enough.' As Miller had predicted. Morg Doyle and his son, Seth. Once-ranchers, the Doyles, but for a long time, worn-heel dealers in anything that promised to turn a dollar and, so it was widely believed, not above laying an iron on a few head of another man's cows or acquiring some of his horses. Opportunists. Never caught at it, though. Until now.

Strickland was in something of a bind. Somehow he needed to put a strong halter on the hard, angry rancher, a man reputed to cling, at least in theory, to the old range custom of stretching the necks of any rustlers found on his range, or beyond it, in possession of any of his animals. That might be a battle yet to come, so Strickland believed.

He said, 'Let's get this clear, Nate. I want 'em taken alive, and I want to take 'em back to Redrock.'

'Some chance!' Besant said. The thickset, squinty man levered a round into the chamber of his Winchester as though to emphasize what he thought about it.

'You hear me too, Jake,' Strickland said. 'Hear what I say in this, or get gone, now.' He turned his face towards the swarthy, unshaven Besant, and managed to include Tex Faulkner in his stare. 'Goes for you, too, Tex.' Strickland now sure wished he had barred them both from riding with him.

Jasper Fox, looking more townified than ever, saw his chance to play the politician, thereby be seen to be *doing the right thing*. Strickland did not welcome the man's support but made no comment when Fox said smoothly, 'Tom's right, boys. County law's got to do it by the book. No other way.' The two hard-nosed men whom Strickland had always felt were closer to Jasper Fox than ought to be the case, fell quiet. Nate Miller looked fit to spit iron, but for the time being, and surprisingly, also held his tongue.

From through the trees the younger of the deputies, Harry Neal, called, 'They're on the move! Climbin' on one horse!'

Strickland, his rifle in one hand, went hurrying between the trees to where his crouching deputies were, but calling to all within earshot,

'Hold fire!' When he got to where he could see clearly the two men in the mouth of the valley, he raised his rifle and let go a whipping shot that was aimed over their heads, but not all that much over them. Startled, both the would-be riders got off the horse and again the animal went trotting away for a short distance, then stopped. To the deputies Strickland said, 'Cover me. That's all.' At once he walked out from the shelter of the trees through long grass and sagebrush, rifle now held in both hands, at his midriff, and kept on walking. Loudly, he called, 'Morg Doyle! Seth! Throw the weapons down! Do it now or by God I'll peg your hides out to dry, right here, inside of ten minutes!' Strickland kept walking. No shot came. The two men were talking animatedly, arguing maybe, watching the inexorably advancing Strickland, knowing who he was, very much aware of the men with him, in cover, probably drawing a bead, only waiting for the command to shoot. And where the horse-stealers were there was only the dead, fly-crawling horse for cover.

When Strickland had taken another four paces, the elder one, Morg Doyle, shouted, 'Hold up there now, Tom!' As though he had not heard, Strickland kept coming. Doyle, the anxiety playing tricks with his voice, called, 'Tell me yuh got a-hold on that there mad bastard Miller!'

Now Strickland stopped. A faint, warm breeze was tugging at his sweat-patched blue shirt.

'Morg, this is my posse. Mine. Nobody gets to do what I don't want 'em to do. Take it or leave it. If you leave it, you've got but a few minutes left to live. So, what's it to be? A prayin' man, are you, Morg?'

Maybe the son, Seth Doyle, would have argued, made an attempt to extract some securities, but the elder man must have known that it was hopeless. He stood up, holding both gloved hands at shoulder level. But he did call, 'By God, Tom, I sure hope your word's good!'

Loudly, Strickland said, 'Seth! Get up on your feet!' A few seconds went by before the skinny son stood up, also raising his hands. Strickland now thought that Seth Doyle's unreadiness to surrender right off had been through fear rather than defiance. Both Doyles, big-eyed to begin with, looked like a pair of bony owls confused by sudden bright daylight. Strickland said, 'Walk on out.' They came stumbling towards him, two gangly, ragged men in range garb, Seth with a wide leather belt pulled tight around his middle and with a pistol in a holster. He was wearing a much soiled, pale-blue shirt and a dented, tall-crowned hat. His pa, black galluses over a grubby grey shirt with no collar, had a pistol stuck down his waistband. While they were approaching, Strickland got the impression that they were trying to make sure that they kept him between themselves and the men waiting in the aspens.

When they got to within a few feet of him, Strickland nodded. They stopped. Dirty, unkempt and very jittery, he could smell them even over his own sweat, and knew that theirs was partly the stench of raw fear. With good reason. They and he would still have to contend with Nate Miller. First, Strickland stepped to Seth Doyle, taking the pistol from its holster. It was an old one, a Walker Colt. Strickland hurled it away. Then he took the pistol, a Remington, from Morg Doyle's waistband and threw it after Seth's Colt.

'Rifles?'

'Up yonder,' Morg said.

The two Warren County deputies, trailed by Miller, Fox, Besant and Faulkner, had by this time emerged from the aspens.

Strickland, looking at the Doyles, made a

15

brief head movement. 'Move.' He had to say it again before they would do it. That their fears were well founded was soon enough confirmed. Miller, his broad face deeply flushed, came striding forward through the lush grass.

'Said it all along! Goddamn' Doyle an' his useless whelp! By God, no bastard lifts what's mine an' walks away! There's on'y one way an' that's to fix it so they cain't never do it agin!'

Strickland turned so that the Winchester, while not pointing directly at the rancher, was not far off it.

'Simmer down, Nate. I'm takin' 'em into Redrock. You want to keep ridin' along, that's fine. Otherwise, go give your boys some help roundin' up your horses an' get on back to the Rocking M.'

Both deputies had turned so that they were facing Miller. Fox, Faulkner and Besant were a couple of yards behind Miller, hesitating, waiting to see what was going to happen. Now, perhaps, it was no longer in Fox's interests to take one side or the other. As Strickland had come to realize long before this, the mood within Warren County, influenced, he believed, by the likes of Jasper Fox, was not running in his own favour. The shadow of his brother, Jack Strickland, seemed even now, at times, to fall across him. There was other personal freight, too, that he carried. The long-ago departure of his wife, Grace. The talk, albeit subdued, about that event and about Jack's woman, of whom some had heard, and what part she might have played in it, before Tom came to Redrock. And about the sporadic eruptions of lawlessness in the county, testing Strickland and testing, therefore, his personal standing with those who had invested in the county. Jasper Fox, for one.

The moment when Nate Miller looked all set to push this affair of the Doyles in Strickland's face, passed. But Strickland knew it was never going to be as easy as that. Yet a call now came that diverted their attention. The Rocking M cowboys were heading back, riding unhurriedly, having rounded up the horses. Miller started gesticulating, and after staring at him for a brief time, they caught on to his meaning. One of the riders went loping away towards the valley where the Doyles had been, and once there, gathered in Morg Doyle's saddled horse.

When they all arrived back at the trees there was some milling around and the Doyles came in for some curious scrutiny and a few jibes. And a shove or two.

Strickland therefore lost no time in getting Morg mounted; then Deputy Neal gave Seth a boost to get him astride the same horse, behind the cantle. Double-mounted as they were, Strickland considered that they needed no special restraints. So within a few minutes, the Redrock posse, with its prisoners and the little bunch of Miller's horses and their attendant riders, set out on the return journey, and at the start, in a brooding silence.

It was not long, however, before Nate

Miller got back to his bellyaching over his horses and the scrawny pair of Doyles riding silently among their enemies.

'Gone soft,' Miller said. 'County. Town. The law. A man kin smell it, all over. One time we druv all the varmints out, them that lived to tell about it. But we went soft, an' now they've all come crawlin' back.' The fact that the Doyles had been around Warren County for a hell of a long time seemed not to support this comment. It was simply that, up to now, they had been too fly for the likes of Nate Miller. But Strickland was aware that what Miller was going on about would find a receptive ear. Jasper Fox, for one, would be listening. Fox was a man who, so Strickland believed, had political ambitions in the county. On the way towards that objective he would much prefer to have his own man put up in Strickland's place. And a particular individual: Brodie Culp, the owner of the Cattleman's saloon; man of property, like Fox himself, who owned several of the stores along Front Street, together with a corral and livery on Haig.

Without making a great play of it, Strickland had Deputy Neal drop back to ride drag, a position from which the often hesitant but generally reliable Neal could keep a wary eye on what was happening. Besant and Faulkner had dropped back to ride with the Rocking M cowhands who were herding the unsaddled horses. Strickland was pleased to see Besant and Faulkner occupied in such a way. Strickland himself was riding on the left side of the prisoners, while Lowell, the feisty, older deputy had taken up a position on the opposite side of them. Miller and Fox were some forty yards ahead.

Presently, in a low voice, the elder Doyle asked, 'Yuh plannin' on stoppin' anywheres 'twixt here an' Redrock?'

'Could be. Why?'

'First chance he gets, that Miller bastard, he's gonna make a try fer us.' Morg Doyle was unable to conceal the fear that Strickland might lose control of this posse. If that were to happen, it could see father and son dancing on the ends of twanging ropes. Strickland knew that it was by no means beyond a possibility, for several times Miller had cast bleak looks over his shoulder at the dejected Doyles, whose guilt he had seen proven beyond all question. And there were five of his riders at his back, as well as the hard men, Faulkner and Besant. Fox? It was impossible to know where Fox might stand. Even if, for the sake of appearances, he could align himself with the law, he could always plead, later, that *the rancher had the numbers.* Fox, the speculator, able to slide either way.

They all rode on. A colder wind was now tugging at them, ruffling the manes and tails of the horses, fluttering bandannas. The prisoners were stoop-shouldered, hunched over and miserable. Briefly, Miller's ruddy face was turned towards them again. Sourly, Strickland wondered if, at the back of their minds, they believed that he was merely making a show of holding Nate Miller in check. For the Doyles had as much, perhaps more, reason to fear him, for it had been their testimony that had freshly indicted his brother, Jack Strickland, and had put his face back on the dodgers. Changed his life. Ruined it. Strickland turned his head and caught Seth Doyle staring at him. The younger Doyle looked quickly away but his expression had been eloquent. Indeed, he thought that Strickland was leading them to their deaths.

Two

Strickland had called a halt to allow the horses a spell. There was some walking around and some pissing and a lighting up of quirlies while the cold wind was tugging at the dismounted riders under a sky that was now densely clouded.

Neal and Lowell were strolling about with apparent idleness, yet never moving far from the silent Doyles, both of whom were now squatting together, sporadically conversing quietly and with their eyes lowered. Maybe it seemed to them that to look up and maybe catch a glance from one of the others in this party might be all that would be needed to have it all turn to shit in jig time.

The Rocking M horses, a poorish lot, so Strickland thought, had been bunched together and were being watched by the cowhands, all young men, these, apart from one, a rheumy-eyed man with a drooping, ragged moustache. When they were not giving their whole attention to the horses, the cowhands were keeping an eye on their employer. Nate Miller was still a most discontented man. At this halt he had chosen to separate himself from the others, and particularly from Strickland and the county deputies, as though, in disgust, he had washed his hands of them. Jasper Fox, the pocked man, Faulkner, and Jake Besant, had formed another detached group some twenty yards from where the Doyles were squatting.

Strickland himself went walking away, flexing his leg muscles, considering lighting up one of his black stogies, then deciding not to. There sure was a continuing uneasiness within this posse as though unseen yet almost palpable waves of malice were coming off it and threatening to engulf it. Fox, Besant and Faulkner were in low conversation, their occasional glances being slid towards Strickland. He had no difficulty in interpreting what the conversation would be about. Rumours had again surfaced concerning Jack Strickland. Older by fourteen years than Tom, long ago in trouble for one reason or another, never able to be settled in his mind after The War Between the States, falling in with a real bad bunch and finishing up in State prison for five years. Spoken of as *the outlaw, Jack Strickland.* Pistolman. Well, State prison had washed away all his sins. Their pa long dead, that episode, the prison, had been the death of their mother. Jack had emerged from behind bars leaner, even harder, withdrawn, and set on vanishing into an anonymous existence. *'Can't go back an' set it all to rights,'* he had said. *'Can't do it all ag'in, neither. Not if it means goin' back in the cage. If I ever did go in agin, Tom, I never will come out.'* He had the grey look that they all had, all the once-jailbirds, as though something of their spirit, of their very essence, had been drained away behind the grim stone walls.

Strickland's narrow-eyed gaze moved from group to group: the ranch riders, the rancher himself, Jasper Fox with the two hard-nosed men, the two deputies, the squatting prisoners. That was where his attention settled, on the Doyles. The Doyles. They had a history that, oddly, was entangled with his own. Well down the Slee River, outside the town of Torrega, heading there to buy stock, so they had claimed, they had had to get out of the way of a bunch of hard-riding men, four of them, set on reaching, so it seemed, the Tessora Hills, and riding as though their asses were afire, men who were yapping sharp words at each other, yapping like over-excited dogs, so one of the Doyles had said. Sweeping by, the Doyles scrambling their horses up in among brush, they had been seen by the urgently riding quartet, but that fact did not cause any of them to turn back. They vanished among thorn brush and juniper, hanging white dust soon the only evidence of their passing.

In Torrega, confused, ashen-faced townsfolk were still trying to come to terms with what had happened. When the Doyles had ridden in, three dead men were still lying in the main street and one other was in the Torrega Bank and Loan, hurt real bad, being attended by a druggist. But that one had lived for only two days. Men wearing canvas masks had come storming into the town about mid-afternoon, to hit the bank. But there had been some unexpected resistance. A lot of shooting. In no time at all, the bandits were pulling out again, empty-handed, leaving the dead and dying.

The Doyles, of course, had been sharply questioned. Some were first inclined to believe that this father and son had in fact been a part of what had gone on. But the Doyles had quickly pointed out the condition of their horses. They showed no signs of hard riding. And anyway, by and by, somebody had recollected that none of the horses ridden by the bandits had looked anything like Seth's buckskin. But in the course of the sharp interrogation, the

Doyles claimed to have heard a name called out between the riders, and that name, so they insisted, had been *Jack*. That had caused no immediate excitement, but when given currency up and down Warren County it had not been long before the name had been joined up with *Strickland*. Out of prison and out of sight for a good long while, it seemed that here he was again, riding with the hard boys. Just like in the past, when his name had been on everybody's lips. Tenuous connection or not, somehow a warrant got issued and dodgers were sent out.

The man now sought was thought to have been living with a woman, Stella Holman, near Indian Creek, but when a posse arrived at that place, headed by the sheriff of Neame County, there had been no sign of Jack Strickland or the woman. Perhaps he had never been there.

That had been about the time that, in Redrock, in Warren County, Tom's wife, Grace Strickland had also departed. For some time there had been talk of a once-association between Stella Holman and Tom, and there had been, perhaps inevitably, talk that in any case Tom knew, or had a damn' good idea, where his brother had gone. In fact Tom Strickland did not know. Nor did he believe that Jack would have been fool enough to get mixed up with the bunch who had tried for the bank in Torrega. Hard man indeed, but that had never been Jack Strickland's style, the random killing. Which did not alter the fact that men, once again, were out looking for Jack Strickland or that Jack had taken what he would have seen as the only course open to him; he had dropped from sight. Certainly, there had been no suggestion that he had ventured across the Warren County line. And the word was that he would never be seen in that county, for there were those who would have relished a situation in which Tom Strickland, by virtue of his sworn office, would have been compelled to take his own brother into custody.

Strickland drew a long breath and headed towards his horse.

'Mount up!'

With some show of reluctance the members of the party drifted to their own mounts, the deputies chivvying the two Doyles along. Miller climbed into the saddle but waited for Strickland to come nearer to him.

'This whole damn' thing sticks in my craw, Strickland.'

'Then you've got your option,' Strickland said, 'an' you know what it is.'

It was unlikely that others had failed to hear the exchange. Indeed, faces were turned towards them expectantly. Nate Miller sure wasn't a man to give up easily. And now he said, 'So yuh gonna shove them two monkeys there in the cage. Yuh'll haul 'em in front of a judge. That fool Mesker, no doubt. Yuh'll git 'em put away fer a time. No ways long enough. All that. Yuh'll throw good county money down the shit-hole. What then? By an' by they'll come weaselin' out an' they'll do the same damn' thing agin.' He was fixing Strickland with a hot stare. 'By God, Strickland, there's a whole lot o' that about, an' if anybody oughta know that, it's you.'

Strickland sat quite still, the wind tugging at the collar of his shirt and ruffling the dark hair bunched thickly at his neck.

'Miller, you'd best explain that to me.' The sudden chill in the tone could not be mistaken. The silence ran on. A horse shifted, whickered. With his knees, Miller nudged his horse and walked it away, Strickland's stare now fixed only on the man's back. Finally Strickland shifted his attention to the prisoners. They were again sitting on their horse in that same hunched-over, defeated attitude, looking down. Faulkner and Besant were eyeing the Doyles too, but with what could only be interpreted as pure malice, and it crossed Strickland's mind that this might he linked to their recent conversation with Fox. Maybe that was where the real pressure was to come from, while Strickland's attention would be expected to be wholly on Nate Miller, for the sombre mood had by no means lifted from this group. The Doyles, too, were very much aware, not only of the atmosphere within the posse but of what lay ahead of them. Plainly they were very leery of Jake Besant and Tex Faulkner, flicking their round-eyed glances towards them even as the whole group now moved on.

The Rocking M cowhands were busy around the recovered horses, and this time, Fox and the two hard-noses were choosing to ride some forty yards behind the group. Strickland would have preferred to have had them out in front where he could have kept an eye on them, but he allowed the matter to rest. There was no point in bringing about further dissent. Miller had joined his men. Strickland, setting the pace, led now, having told his deputies to track closely the horse the prisoners were on.

They came to an area dominated by red rock buttes and where there were large clumps of brush, and the posse became for a time somewhat strung out. What possessed the Doyles to think they could get away with bolting from the men who had them, it would be impossible to guess, yet bolt they did, plunging between tall brush and soon passing from view. Fear, as Strickland thought later, will do strange things to men, driving them beyond the borders of reason. Yet his mind went racing ahead of the event.

He yelled at his deputies, 'Get after 'em! But I want 'em back *alive!*' Even as he shouted at the deputies he was unscabbarding his rifle and getting his startled horse turned around. The sudden move by the Doyles had taken everybody by surprise. Nate Miller happened to be across on the opposite side of his gather of horses. At this stage Fox, Faulkner and Besant had been trailing by more than eighty yards, but now all three came bounding forward, and Strickland caught the glint of rifles being grabbed from scabbards. He steadied the big bay beneath him and raised one gloved hand. 'Hold up! Hold up! Leave it to the deputies!' The three riders kept coming. Miller could be heard, shouting something and the rancher was hauling his horse around, apparently to join the Fox group as they came by. Strickland acted on impulse and sent a rifle shot lashing over the heads of the Rocking M horses and their drovers. At once there was some confusion, several of the animals breaking away. Miller yelled at Strickland but checked his horse, his attention now diverted.

Strickland headed directly towards the on-coming Fox, Faulkner and Besant. For the space of a few seconds he thought that they would take no heed of him, but Fox said something and all three arrived on pranc-ing, side-stepping horses to front Strick-land, no more than five yards from him.

Fox asked, 'What the hell's got into you, Tom?' Fox's face was flushed with annoy-ance, his customary calmness absent.

Strickland said, 'The deputies, they'll soon

enough run 'em down. An' they'll take 'em alive.'

Faulkner could not sit on his anger, bringing his horse forward, even bumping Strickland's bay, rifle held high in one hand. 'By God, Strickland, tell us jes' where yuh stand in this?' He, too, came shoving in close.

Besant, ever ready to side Faulkner, threw in an answer. 'Where any goddamn' Strickland would stand, that's where!'

So there it was, as blatantly laid out as it was possible to be. The link with Jack Strickland. The outlaw. The Torrega killer. Having been goaded already by Miller on that issue and now more deliberately insulted on the same matter, Strickland had had enough; and in particular, hearing it from the likes of Jake Besant.

'You've got a mouth that's full of shit, Jake. As I recall, you always did have. An' nothing to back it up.'

Instant fury brought a deep crimson crawling across Besant's face, and that same fury was enough to push him into a rash act.

He swung the barrel of the rifle at Strickland. Strickland swayed in the saddle, only just managing to avoid being struck full in the face. Recovering fast, he drove the barrel of his own rifle at Besant, catching him high on the chest. As Besant cried out and swayed in the saddle, Strickland bumped his horse in against Besant's mount and whacked a gloved fist to the side of the other rider's jaw. Besant slumped over on the far side of the horse and the animal went jumping sideways. Besant then came clear of the stirrups and fell from the saddle, thumping heavily onto the ground.

Fox and Faulkner shouted and both began crowding forward, only to be confronted by Strickland's rifle.

'Ease up there, boys...' From a distance came the sound of a rifle shot, but whoever had let it go was lost somewhere among the brush. Besant, shaking his head, seemed now to be trying to retrieve his rifle. Strickland said, 'You never learn, Jake. Try for it, mister, an' I'll nail you.' Lower lip bloodied, Besant squinted up at Strickland.

Fox said, 'It's come to a fine pass, Tom, when there's a fallin' out among a posse.'

'Not my doing,' said Strickland. 'There's things I'll swallow an' things I won't. Jake's a fool, an' he crossed the line.'

Nate Miller's voice called, 'What in the name o' God's goin' on?'

Strickland ignored the call, still giving his whole attention to Faulkner and Fox. From a distance he could hear some shouting, then presently the sounds of some horses coming. Somewhere behind him the yipping, whistling cowhands were still occupied, regathering Miller's bunch of horses. And now, out of the brush came the deputies, flanking the double-mounted Doyles, these two looking very hang-dog and apprehensive indeed.

'Had to put one over their hats,' Lowell said. So that explained the rifle shot. Lowell and Neal were looking at the dismounted Besant who was in a bent-forward attitude, one hand held to the side of his jaw.

'Had me some problems here, too,' said Strickland, 'but they've been taken care of.' Whatever happened now – and Strickland thought that there would be no further pressure put on him between here and Redrock – this would probably come to be seen as the true beginning of his problems as the Warren County sheriff. To Besant, he said, 'Get back up in that saddle, Jake. Put the rifle back on the horse. Raise your hand to me again, here or anywhere else, an' I'll bust your thick head open.' Strickland shuffled his horse around, scabbarding his own rifle, and moved away, waving the deputies and their prisoners ahead of him. But to Nate Miller, he called,

'Soon as we get to Jared Bluff, take your boys an' your horses an' head on back to your outfit.' He did not wait for a reply.

Fox's eyes bored into Strickland's back. Faulkner, still holding his rifle, looked once at Fox. Fox shook his head. He might just as well have said, however, *'Not this time. But the time'll come.'*

Three

Ten miles short of Redrock, when Strickland looked back, Miller, his men and his horses had fallen a long way behind. It seemed that Strickland's advice to the rancher had been accepted, however grudgingly, so now there was only Fox, Faulkner and Besant to keep a wary eye on. It eased his mind to a certain extent, for which he was thankful, for he was tired and simply wished to get this task over and then get some sleep. And on the morrow other duties awaited him. So about an hour later he was relieved to see against the low-clouded sky, the rise of the roofs of Redrock.

The town of Redrock was reasonably large. It was also a somewhat haphazard place. There was a lengthy main street but some of the off-streets, and others, occasionally petered out among miscellanies of wooden structures of all kinds. If Redrock could have been viewed from above it would have revealed itself as a conglomeration of buildings, many smaller buildings, large barns, several corrals, weed-strewn lots scattered among all manner of busy enterprises, a railroad depot and water tower and a yard with multiple steel tracks and a large locomotive shed together with a huddle of other railroad buildings, all of which were painted a dusty red colour.

When the remains of Strickland's posse got back into town, dismounted the prisoners and led them quickly in through the county office to the cages at the back, it did not take long for word to get around. No doubt Faulkner, Besant and Jasper Fox would have had plenty to do with that for they had all headed on down Front Street, presumably to Brodie Culp's saloon, the Cattleman's.

Certainly it was not long before the

mayor, John Straker, put in an appearance at the county office, came bustling in through the front door in his brown ulster and his derby hat. A short, round man, Straker.

'Well, Sheriff Strickland, a good result. A good result.' Yet it sounded like something studied, being said as a matter of form.

'So far,' Strickland said. The deputies were clattering around, stowing rifles in a gun-rack. 'It's all yet to go through due process.' Then he said, 'I've got to say that Nate Miller's none too pleased.' He stopped short of saying that Miller, in the throes of his deep anger, had been all for stringing the Doyles up. That would be bound to reach the mayor's ears in due course.

'Nate's a man that can get riled up real easy,' Straker conceded, apparently un-aware, or unconcerned, that he was ludicrously understating reality. And soon enough Straker would get to hear of other matters to do with the Strickland posse and would not like what he heard. Then, as

Strickland had expected, Straker said, 'A swift finish to this here, er, business would sure be applauded by the Merchants' an' Cattlemen's Guild.'

'It'll be as quick or as slow as the judiciary makes it,' Strickland said. 'That's something that's out of my hands.'

'Of course,' Straker said. 'Of course, Tom.' Tom. Friendly. Strickland reflected that whenever the Redrock mayor Tom'd him it was intended to advance an assurance of goodwill, of man-to-man understanding, a sense of *'I know how difficult your job can be'*. In the present circumstances that would endure for as long as Straker was not in possession of all the facts. The sole element of relief, right now, was that Strickland was being spared the lecture on the necessity for a perceived stability in Warren County generally and the town of Redrock in particular, insofar as business investment was concerned. Like Jasper Fox, John Straker, together with members of the Merchants' and Cattlemen's Guild, was something of a speculator, principally in land, but also in railroad and other stock. Yet no matter what Straker might say to him in this office, Strickland knew that the man's words had no true substance. It would soon be a different matter if Strickland's next action should run counter to Straker's personal agenda. Indeed, Strickland believed that the mayor stood already among those who were anxious to see a change in the office of Warren County Sheriff. Strickland was unsure, however, whether or not Straker actually supported Brodie Culp for that job. Straker, by his very nature, was at heart a politician, so you never knew what he was really thinking, which way he might jump. For Strickland it could all unravel real quick.

After Straker left the office, the deputies, too, went out, only to return shortly afterwards, looking concerned.

Lowell said, 'Could be we got us a problem, Tom.' Strickland had become aware that there were numerous people gathered near the county building. He assumed that this was what Lowell meant. It wasn't.

'Jes' seen Nate Miller.'

'Where?' Strickland's question was immediate and there was an edge to his tone.

'Down to Edgecumbe's Corral.'

'On his own?'

'Far as we seen.'

'Nate catch sight of you?'

Lowell shrugged. 'Cain't say fer sure.'

Harry Neal went to the grimy window. 'Nate's right across the street there now, talkin'.'

Strickland and Lowell moved across to take a look. There, indeed, was the rancher, outside a freight office and surrounded by a group of maybe a dozen men, and indeed Miller was talking animatedly. Strickland wearily passed a rough hand across his face. This, he did not need.

Lowell said, 'I kin go out an' give 'em the word, Tom. Clear 'em all away.'

'No.' Strickland shook his head. 'Go take a look down back. Make sure those boys are settled.' And to Harry Neal, 'Can't stop Nate from talkin'. An' he's way across the street. But this lot just here, our side, step out an' move 'em on.' Deliberately Strickland had avoided sending the more testy of his deputies, Jase Lowell, onto a street where, soon, some sharp words might have to be exchanged. There could be no point in actively provoking trouble. Yet he knew that the situation, over the next hour or two, could turn sour, particularly if certain parties got down to some serious drinking. It would not be long 'til sundown.

Neal did not take a rifle down from the gunrack but merely put his hat back on and went easing on out through the front doorway onto the boardwalk. When he got there, curious faces were turned towards him. Without raising his voice unduly, Neal cleared his throat and said, 'Nothin' at all to see here, gents. Best yuh leave. Go home.'

One bystander said, 'There's plenty places

45

that'd see the likes o' them Doyles git their chicken necks stretched, an' fer a whole less'n what they done!'

'Mebbe. But in this here county, them days is gone, friend.' Righteous in his office, Neal was repeating, now, what Strickland had often observed. 'It's laid down. There's got to be due process. That's what the law says.'

As it turned out, there was no real argument. The small crowd began dispersing. But Nate Miller, followed by others, came pacing across the dry street. Loudly, Miller said, 'Wherever Tom Strickland's hidin', boy, you go tell him this from me: I still ain't gonna sit still fer this!'

Neal said, possibly surprising himself, 'Yuh got all o' yore hosses back, Mr Miller, an' we got the varmints that took 'em. An' fer now, that's the end of it.'

Miller, florid and testy, unaccustomed to being thwarted in any of his dealings, said, 'Don't yuh be too sure o' that, boy! That there tin badge yuh got pinned on, it's made yuh kinda cocky. But I ain't fergot yuh ain't nothin' but a two-bit cow-puncher turned lawman, an' when it suits, I kin spit out two-bit cow-punchers.'

Neal, reddening, his confidence suddenly reduced in the face of the rancher's truths was unaware how he might proceed. But at his back there was a sound, and Strickland stepped out of the office.

'I've never hid from any man, Nate. I'd have picked you to know better than that. Now you hear me: I've got me some prisoners inside here. They're men that are being held by this county on a charge of theft. They'll get their day in court. We'll all be there, an' you'll be entitled to come. In fact, you'll have no choice. No doubt you'll be called as a prosecution witness. What, happens after that will be up to the court. Right now I'd advise you to simmer down an' ride back out to the Rocking M.'

'I'll ride when an' where I see fit, Strickland! I rid with your goddamn' posse, no less! An' they was my hosses that was stole!'

'Well, like Deputy Neal said, you got 'em all back. I've got the men that stole 'em, so now it's my problem until such time as it gets to be the court's problem.'

'Blind waste! Good county money!' Miller was truly angry. But from the start he must have known that a show of aggression would be all that it could amount to. The rancher turned and went pushing his way back through the small group that had come across the street with him. Strickland heard the escape of a long breath from Harry Neal.

'Sure glad to see the ass-end o' that man,' Neal said.

'Nate's last bluster,' Strickland said. He sure hoped it would be. He went back inside. Neal followed him in. In the greyness of oncoming night he got ready to light the lantern above the door of the county office. Lowell, too, had come back up and was now lighting the office lamps.

He said, 'I'll go on down an' fetch some chow fer them two bastards.'

Strickland nodded. Neal had lit the lantern and came back in. Strickland reminded them that in the morning he would be heading to Tressida and would return on the following day.

To Neal he said, 'Best you go get some shuteye. Come back in five, six hours an' let Jase go. I'll bunk down here. Whoever's around, boot me awake before sun-up.' And to Lowell, he said, 'I doubt that Nate Miller'll be back, not 'til the court hearing. The Doyles, they'll have to be represented. Gif Noakes might do it. Ask 'em about it, an' if they agree, ask Gif. The county will prosecute with Dan Lemuel. No doubt he'll want access, too.' Strickland was very tired. He had thought of talking with the Doyles himself but discarded the idea. He did ask, 'They got light up there?' When Lowell nodded, 'Go get the chow an' don't forget to enter the cost. An' keep a close eye on 'em.' Earlier, Strickland had fetched his bedroll and blanket in, and now he walked through into an ante-room where there was a bare cot which sometimes was used by the off-duty deputy. Strickland took off his boots and socks and lay down, almost immediately sliding into sleep.

The streets of Redrock, lit intermittently by lanterns hung on long, rough poles and with numerous lamplit windows relieving the many other corners of velvet dark, seemed reluctant for some time to yield to the hours of night. Maybe it was the events of the late afternoon, the return of the Strickland posse with its subdued, down-at-heel prisoners, and the visible anger of the rancher, Miller, that had developed a feeling of deep unease. The saloons were open but oddly low-key; the DeLange Hotel – so called – on the edge of the town near the railroad yards, where the whores were, had many of its lamps lit but – or so it seemed – there was not nearly as much to-ing and fro-ing as usual. The brick courthouse with its white flagpole out front, stood in darkness. The mayor and some members of the citizens' council of Redrock had met in an informal way at Straker's large frame house on Adamson; and the attorneys had been in and out of the county office. Deputy Lowell was in that office now, his hat tossed on a desk, he leaning back in a creaking swivel chair, his boots resting on another straight-backed chair arranged for the purpose.

Strickland came fumbling out of sleep, disturbed by loud noises, some of which were being made by Lowell running along the passageway to the cells. Somebody was shouting, and Strickland was sure that what had jolted him from sleep had been a gunshot. By the time his feet touched the floor he was certain that most of the yelling was coming from the prisoners. By the time he had emerged, barefoot, into the passage-way, Lowell, having been down at the cells, was returning.

'Seth Doyle's been shot. He ain't all that bad. Some mounted feller musta come down the alley an' let go on the fly.' It was true that a horseman would have been high enough to get a look inside the cells through any of the barred windows at the side of the jail. 'I'll go on down an' fetch one o' the docs, or Seth, he never will quit his goddamn' caterwaulin'.'

Certainly the noises coming from the low-lit cell had shown no signs of ceasing. Strickland went back into the ante-room and put on socks and boots, then visited the cells.

His prisoners were wide-eyed and clearly very rattled, Seth still making a good deal of noise, blood streaked across the side of his face where he had been raked by the bullet. It had been a near thing, but as Lowell had claimed, Seth had not been badly hurt. The man was, however, scared near out of his wits. Abruptly Strickland told him to shut up or find out what being hurt really was. This had some effect but Seth still went on complaining, albeit in a quieter tone

The elder Doyle said, 'By God, Strickland, it's come to somethin' when a man cain't git no protection from the law no more!'

'That's got a real strange sound, coming

from you, Morg,' Strickland said. 'But I'll have the pair of you shifted to a cage on the other side of the building. Can't give you any guarantees but it'll be a mite safer.'

'Yuh won't have far to look,' Doyle said, 'to locate the men that done this. Git that mad bastard Miller arrested an' we'll be safe enough.'

'There's no proof it was Miller,' said Strickland. Seth, a hand held to his bleeding face supplied a whining response to that. 'Who the hell else would it be?'

Nonetheless, the Doyles exchanged glances, prompting Strickland to observe, 'You'd know that a whole lot better than I would. This county's not exactly crawling with friends of yours.' The Doyles thereupon fell quiet.

The doctor who arrived with Deputy Lowell was a tall, well-built man named George Halliburton. Already apprised of what had happened, he nodded to Strickland, was admitted to the cell and there spent some fifteen minutes attending to

Seth Doyle's injury. After Halliburton had departed, Strickland did have the pair moved to a cell on the other side of the building where there was much less space for a horseman to approach. And this time no lamp was lit in the cell. To Lowell, he said, 'Leave the one burning in the other cage.' The lethal moth that had been drawn to it earlier might just come fluttering back for another try. But such was not to be the case.

Before sun-up Strickland was in the saddle and heading for Tressida. By mid-afternoon he was walking his horse along the main street of that place towards the Wilson House Hotel where he would pay for a room for the night. This afternoon and evening, however, he was to meet with a justice of the peace named Trengrove.

The events he had left behind him in Redrock were still matters of concern to him. Had he been able to order his affairs differently he would not have come as far as Tressida at this time. As soon as the doctor had attended Seth Doyle and the prisoners had been shifted within the county jail, he had left Lowell guarding them and had himself taken a good look all around the county building. He had not expected to find anything of significance and did not. Then he had gone seeking Nate Miller. The rancher had still been in Redrock and eventually Strickland had discovered him playing faro in Brodie Culp's saloon. There had ensued a brief and angry exchange when Strickland had asked his blunt questions, but the plump little man, Culp, had informed Strickland that *Mr Miller* had been in his company all through the evening. Strickland had left the saloon but not before Nate Miller had had to be restrained by others.

Strickland knew that his visit and the loud argument that it had provoked would have done his present standing in Redrock no good, particularly as the man, Culp, had first been on the fringes, and then had become involved in it. At every turn it seemed that if his own reading was accurate, he was losing ground in public opinion. And no matter what Mayor Straker had said after the bringing in of the Doyles, Straker inescapably was a politician, and as such an opportunist plain and simple. Moreover, the mayor was a man of some influence and he would set a course that would be of advantage to himself and his supporters. Strickland, no matter what his record in the past, if the mood so dictated, would be swept aside in favour of someone seen as being more malleable. And Strickland believed that the re-emergence of the rumours about his brother had not come about by accident.

For no immediate reason his wife, Grace, long gone back East, came to his mind. There again, talk had had her departure linked to the name of Jack Strickland's woman, Stella Holman. Doubtless there were women in Redrock who liked to see themselves as moral gatekeepers of the community, who still remembered that covert talk and thought the less of Strickland because of it. Truth would never enter the evaluation. It had been the stresses and tensions of this raw life out here that had eventually become unbearable for Grace.

He met with Trengrove and spent tedious but necessary hours going through papers, affidavits and statements to be lodged with the court, all precursors to legal proceedings, mostly over land. Then with a sense of relief Strickland made his way back to the Wilson House.

When he got there a telegram was waiting for him. It was from Deputy Lowell. The Doyles had been busted out of jail. Neal had been hurt and both of the Doyles had been shot. Seth Doyle was dead.

Four

If the people of Redrock had been disturbed by what had happened at the county office, and afterwards, there was little evidence today, on the main street of the town. Activities seemed to be going on in much the same way as usual as Strickland hitched the bay horse to the tie rail, then went across the boardwalk and stepped inside the office. Lowell was in there and so too was the younger of the deputies, Neal. A starkly white gauze bandage was wrapped around his head. His face was pale, seemingly bloodless. Neal was sitting in the swivel chair behind the desk. When Strickland came in he would have got to his feet but Strickland waved him down again. Some indeterminate sounds were coming from somewhere down in the cells. Strickland merely raised his eyebrows.

Lowell said, 'Doc Halliburton's still up there with Morg Doyle.' Then as though he thought that wanted more explanation, 'There warn't nowheres else to take Morg. Well, no bastard wanted him.'

Strickland took his hat off and tossed it on the desk among a mess of papers. 'How bad is he?'

'Real bad. Jes' been up there an' took me a look. Doc don't put any money on Morg comin' through it.'

Strickland drew a long breath. 'Better tell me what happened.'

Harry Neal in a somewhat strained voice, said, 'I was in here. Jase was home. 'Bout seven I called Larsen's boy over an' had him fetch supper in fer me an' fer the Doyles. Come near to eight I was gittin' ready fer Jase to come in an' take over. Then these two fellers come easin' in. Not much noise nor nothin'. Canvas masks. They was holdin' pistols. Me, I didn't have no chance. Never even heeard the bastards comin'.

They had the drop. They took the keys, an' when we was all down to the cells one o' the bastards laid a barrel on me. Don't recall nothin' after that.'

It crossed Strickland's mind that the other deputy, Lowell, had been leaving it somewhat late to come in to relieve Neal but he let that pass. It was Lowell who said, 'They musta scared the Doyles real bad, I reckon. Not a peep out of 'em.'

'Two of 'em,' Strickland said. 'Masked. Nobody on the street saw anything? Heard anything?'

'Nope. Nobody we've found, anyways.' Lowell was scraping at the stubble on his jaw. 'Took the pair of 'em out real quiet. Mounts 'round in the alley, so it 'ppears. By the time I come in it was all over. Harry, he was tryin' to git on his feet. He fell down agin. I went an' got Doc Earl. When he come I got a-holt of a few o' the boys. It took a while, but we lit out lookin' fer sign.'

'At night. Which direction?'

Lowell licked dry lips. 'Grover Spade, he

was in the party. We figured they'd mebbe cut sou'-west, head fer the Tessora Hills. Grover, he found fresh horse apples an' some other sign about five hunnert yards out. Coupla mile further on we heeard a lot o' shots goin' off. Then we run across a saddled hoss on the loose. We catched it.'

'Brand?'

Lowell sniffed. 'Rockin' M.' Then, 'Coulda been stole.'

'It could. You talked with Miller about it?'

'Nope. Not yet. Nate's back to his spread, so I hear.'

Strickland nodded. 'Then what?'

'We rid on a quarter-mile. Less, mebbe. We come on the Doyles. They was on the ground an' on their own. No sign o' no hosses. No sign o' them masked fellers. Seth, he was plain daid, half o' his face shot off an' bullet holes in his shirt. Jeez, he was some mess! Morg, he'd been shot bad three, four times but he was still breathin'. Reckoned we couldn't leave Morg out there while somebody rode fer a doc. We put 'im acrost the hoss we'd catched an' brung 'im in. Fetched Seth in over the same hoss.'

Strickland thought that if Morg Doyle hadn't been real bad to start with, he sure would have been by the time they got him back to Redrock across a horse. There was a step and a rustle of clothing as Doc Halliburton appeared from the direction of the cells.

'No good I'm afraid, gentlemen. The man is dead. He'd lost too much blood, and by my assessment there were severe internal injuries.'

Strickland asked, 'Was he conscious at any point?'

'In and out of consciousness,' said Halliburton.

'Did he say anything?'

The doctor hesitated. Then, 'Nothing I could make head or tail of.' Halliburton hefted his leather bag. 'There'll have to be an autopsy of course.'

'Not here, I hope,' said Strickland.

'No. Oh no. He can be taken straight to

Lacey's parlour, where the – where his son is.' Halliburton gave Strickland a probing look. 'Redrock is getting to be a quite violent place, Mr Strickland.'

Strickland said nothing. Halliburton's tone suggested a certain criticism directed at himself. The doctor then left, nodding briefly to all present. To his deputies, Strickland said, 'There's certain to be a whole lot of questions about this. If you get pinned down by folks, tell 'em to come talk to me. There'll be an inquiry – an inquest. People will have to wait for that.' Then, 'Whoever it was took those boys out of here didn't want to kill 'em in the jail. Didn't want to shoot pistols off an' have people come running in jig time. That's why they took 'em out quiet an' rode a couple of miles out.'

'Nate Miller's gonna have some questions to answer,' Lowell said. He looked very sour.

Strickland said, 'Leave Nate to me.' He would talk to Miller but he was not looking forward to it. Almost accused over the earlier attack on the Doyles, Miller would no doubt be furious at another visit. Yet Strickland knew that he could not simply allow the matter to lapse, not follow up the one fact that they had. The brand. Yet Strickland realized that he would have plenty of questions to answer himself. Some of them were not long in being asked and came to him in the shape of John Straker. At the time, Strickland was alone in the office.

'Sheriff Strickland, this here is a terrible business. It's got this entire community real shook up. Men taken right out of the county jail. One shot dead, the other real bad–?

'Dead,' Strickland said. 'Morg Doyle's dead.'

'My God!' Then, 'Sheriff, people are going to be wantin' answers. They'll be askin' how come masked men come walkin' right in here an' then right out agin with county prisoners, an' why they got shot. An' who it was carried out these here murders. An' what business it was that couldn't wait, took you, Sheriff Strickland, miles away, when there's only two deputies on hand to, er, watch the shop.'

Controlling his anger, Strickland said, 'I'll answer the last one first. My responsibilities don't begin an' end here in Redrock. Due process has to take place elsewhere, too. In this case it happened to be Tressida. If I hadn't gone, an' yesterday, that would have gotten me in more trouble with the judiciary than you or I could handle. Yeah, the timing was kind of unfortunate the way things turned out, but that couldn't be helped. Second, whoever had been in here wouldn't have stood a chance. Neal was the unlucky one. He was hit real hard. It could've killed Harry. The Doyles, they're dead, I reckon, because somebody couldn't afford to let 'em live. Who did it? That's what I've got to try to find out.'

Straker, under his derby, was regarding him stonily. 'As I understand it, Nate Miller threatened 'em. He wanted 'em strung up.'

'Nate Miller's one of the old-timers. We all

know it. He'll make threats to get his own way an' he's not got out of some old habits.'

Straker could see that he was getting nowhere pursuing this line, but he said, 'Things like this have got a bad habit of sparkin' others. That's what's startin' to get at folks here, Sheriff. There's a feelin' that we're losin' our grip on things. That's bad. That's a real bad thing in a community. Makes folks real jittery.'

Strickland could see well enough the way it was heading but chose not to prolong a discussion that he had not wanted in the first place. It would be fruitless. Straker had really come in here to deliver a particular message and now he had got that done. What that meant, of course, was that this entire matter had been discussed, first maybe, behind closed doors and then, inevitably, more widely, and that he, Strickland, was at the centre of it. Again he sensed strongly the hand of Jasper Fox, no doubt promoting the notion of Brodie Culp as the new chief law officer of Warren County.

Straker gone, Strickland watched as the body of Morg Doyle, covered by a grey blanket and laid on a canvas stretcher, was carried by an assistant of the undertaker, Lucius Lacey, and Deputy Lowell, out of the county building and along to Lacey's parlour by an alley-and-backstreet route. Strickland wished to engage as little public interest as possible in the proceedings. Strickland himself walked outside. He had a small task to carry out involving Wells, Fargo, needing to talk with the agent there. He met Lowell who was on his way back from Lacey's parlour and told the deputy where he was heading. Lowell carried on back to the county office.

Strickland did not get as far as Wells, Fargo. Up ahead of him, on the same side of the street as Wells, Fargo, stood a saloon called the Royal Flush. Clearly some sort of disturbance was taking place, much shouting and some smashing sounds like furniture being destroyed. Strickland lengthened his stride and settled his hat more firmly on his head. This was an unusually early hour for a saloon brawl but that was sure what it sounded like.

Before he reached the place the batwing doors burst open and a man came staggering out, backwards, across the boardwalk and crashed into the tie rail where the four horses there tugged at their secured reins and worked their heads up and down in alarm. The man fell to his knees, a range rider by the look of his clothing, moleskin pants, leather chaps and a collarless, grey-wool shirt. As he went crawling away, hatless head drooping, bleeding, another man emerged, this one a bony individual wearing a ragged brown shirt and narrow black pants tucked into long, well-scuffed boots. Clearly he had been drinking hard, his narrow face flushed and an unsteadiness about him. Drunk but dangerous, for in his right hand was a cocked pistol.

The first thing Strickland did was yell at him to get his attention, for the pistol, though wavering, was coming up to centre on the cowhand who was still crawling along the boardwalk. The unsteady man turned, his mouth agape, staggered slightly, straightened and brought his gunhand around much quicker than Strickland had expected. Too late, he realized that he was not yet close enough to jump in and grab the man's right arm. Even as this realization came to him he was drawing his own Colt pistol. It was touch and go. As Strickland's pistol went off in a flash and rush of smoke, the other man's weapon flared but the lead went tearing through the awning directly above Strickland's head. The drunken man was whacked and he spun around, his pistol dropping as he fell to the boardwalk. The acrid stench of gunsmoke and the haze of it was all about Strickland as he put his pistol away and went forward. The entire action had occupied only a matter of seconds.

The drunken pistolman was alive but in obviously bad shape, the right shoulder of his brown shirt bloodied and with a black bullet hole in it. The shot man was writhing in pain and beginning to make a lot of noise. Men were emerging from the saloon. Others were coming from various other places, for plainly the shooting was over. One of those who came was Doc Earl, carrying his bag. At once Earl called for the gathering crowd to give him some space so he could get a look at the man who had been shot. The other, the cowhand who had come crashing out through the batwings, had got to his feet and was going unsteadily away. Strickland made no move to stop him, and instead, of the bystanders, asked about the man now being examined by Earl.

'Who is he?'

Nobody knew. Not a Redrock man, nor a known rider from any of the outlying ranches. Not a Rocking M rider, anyway, which, so Strickland thought, was something. Over Earl's shoulder, Strickland took a look at the man.

Earl said, 'I need to have this man moved carefully away from here. He's in a bad way. He's got to be taken to my surgery.' He turned his head and gave Strickland a look that could have meant anything, then looked away. Men had gone hurrying to fetch a stretcher. Strickland turned and walked away. Lowell was there.

Strickland said, 'No chance to do anything else. No chance.'

All along the main street there had fallen an almost eerie quiet, most of the men and women and horses and wagons seemingly standing where all of them had stopped at the moment that the pistols had gone off.

On the following day the man Strickland had shot, the entire joint of the right shoulder destroyed, died in Earl's back room. Shock as much as the awful gunshot wound, so Earl reported.

Five

They were still at the smallholding which, a long time back, had belonged to some kin of Stella Holman. Her and Jack Strickland. Uncertainty was hanging in the very air, yet with it now, a growing acceptance of the inevitable.

A tall, gaunt man, Jack Strickland had aged beyond his years. The time he had endured in State prison had sure left its mark. So, too, had the wild years before that came to pass. And when, after a time of freedom, his sentence served, he had been compelled to go to ground again, travelling with Stella to live at this remote place down on the Slee River, his days had become a succession of bleak and watchful episodes, Jack Strickland unable to move far, yet, to work the farm at all, needing to take some risks. As the weeks had become months and the months had added up to almost a year, they had even dared hope that they had got away with it, that he would be able to live out his life in that place, his name eventually to be forgotten, the curling yellowed reward dodgers long buried beneath others. Now that hope had all turned to shit. They must get on the move again, always casting glances over their shoulders. All because of a man whom Jack had got wind of: Rudolph Stone.

Strickland, seeking to market farm produce, had visited a town called Helena, deep in the shadows of the Tessora Hills where there were men who themselves owned dubious histories and in whom Strickland felt he could put some degree of trust. That was how he had come to learn of Stone.

To Stella he said, 'A few years back there was a rumour that that particular bastard was dead. Somewhere up near the Canadian border.'

Stella sat down slowly, her large, dark eyes fixed on him. 'Can you be sure it's him? That they've got it right?'

'The man I had it from saw him an' had a drink with him in Sharp's Ferry. No, there's no doubt it was him.'

'Sharp's Ferry. But that's more than a hundred miles from here.' Yet she could see that he was seriously worried. Maybe, even after all this time together he was not telling her everything. But all the signs were that he believed what he had been told and it had shaken him severely. He looked remote, hunched, defensive. Perhaps for the first time in a long while, he was afraid. She studied him as he paced up and down. Gaunt. Like some ravaged bird of prey driven down from the heights through hunger. Now, however, this man, this Rudolph Stone, had become the bird of prey. As Jack Strickland paced, his face a taut mask, her eyes were still following him sadly. She knew that it was pointless to persist with questions, *How can we know he's headed down here? How do we know it's you he's looking for? Or that he's looking for anybody?* Such questions would only push him over into anger. He was older now and, like her, tired of running. Yet now, all the old demons were gathering at his shoulder. And at hers. Without warning the image of his brother, Tom, came to Stella, almost causing her to take a sharp draw of breath. Soon, if it had not already happened, the brother's name would come to Jack's mind, too. If they were compelled to pull out of here, leave this small farm behind them, they might have to head along the line of the Slee River so that they might then make a wide loop around that part of the country where Jack Strickland would believe Stone to be coming from. That, inescapably, would take them closer than Jack would like to Warren County. Tom's jurisdiction. Stepping across that line could put his brother in a terrible position, Tom having to hunt him down. For Jack's presence would be certain to be discovered sooner or later.

One bleak night in the past, long before State prison, listening at a partly open door, she had heard Jack saying, *'I never will throw a shadow anywhere near yuh. I'll never push yuh into a goddam' corner like that.'* Jack Strickland had kept resolutely to his word.

Carefully, she now asked him, 'Do we really need to leave here? Is that what it'll come to?'

For a little time she thought that he had not heard her. Then he said, 'I could stand an' wait fer the bastard. But he'd have it all in his favour. I couldn't never sleep. Yeah, we got to go, Stella. We got to go now.' Then, 'If Stone's on the move, the word'll be out, all over. Talk. Rumours. Enough to stir folks up, all over.' What he did not say, did not need to, for she would have thought of it already, was, *Maybe Tom will get to hear.* And that would go off like a cannon in Warren County.

The moment when she could have said, *I'm not moving,* came and went. It had been no more than the blink of an eye. She stood up. 'How much stuff can we take?'

'Whatever we can get aboard a couple of pack animals.' Two of the farm horses. Answering her unspoken question, he said, 'The other two, we'll have to turn loose.' It meant, too, that most of her possessions would have to be abandoned. Yet there had really been no question but that she would go with him. Anyway, there were some who already knew where Jack Strickland had been, these past months. She did not want to be alone here when Stone came, as she knew in her heart he would.

In less than two days' time they found themselves not quite in Warren County but in the north-western corner of its neighbour, Somes County, and specifically in the dreary, ramshackle town of Dorelia. At one time a centre for alluvial mining that had been carried on along that part of the Slee, the boom days – such as they had been – had vanished long ago. Not much of anything in Dorelia now, and during the years of decline it had missed out on getting even a spur of the railroad. Like the far-off town of Helena, where Jack Strickland had got wind of Rudolph Stone, Dorelia was shadowed by the Tessora Hills, whose pine-covered slopes, topped with tall firs, it seemed possible to reach out and touch.

Dorelia was indeed no longer a place of any account. Those who came to it from somewhere were all heading to somewhere else, never tarrying in the town for longer than was necessary. No lawman resided there. Not much more than a way station now, but one saloon managing to stay open for business. A half-dozen others were boarded up. A clapped-out store was still trading; there was a corral and a hotel where stage passengers sometimes paused while waiting to transfer from one stage-line to another.

Jack Strickland and Stella Holman went to the hotel, the name of which they did not know, since the painted sign had been sand-scoured and obliterated. Their saddlers and pack-animals they had lodged in Standeven's Corral and Livery. Given his way, Strickland would not have ventured near Dorelia but Stella had protested that she was too tired to continue.

They were in a musty upstairs room, Strickland having had to prowl around to locate somebody to hire it to them. Finally he had flushed out of a back room a fat, dead-eyed woman who had seemed manifestly indifferent but had handed over a key in exchange for payment upfront. Soon, now, they would go out to the one café, they had noticed on the way in, for Stella said there was no way she would sit down to a meal in this dump. But there was a discussion to be had first.

'Where to from here? Which direction?'

He had been giving it almost constant thought and had come to the conclusion that he did not like the course which seemed the best insofar as safety was concerned. He said, 'We could cross the Slee at Jacob's Ford an' move into the Tessora Hills. Slow goin' but once across we'd be in the clear.'

Stella was over near the single window, the stained shade partly raised, looking down onto the rutted, weedy main street. Tired she might be, and showing it, yet he thought how trim she was in her denim shirt and slim-waisted, divided riding skirt. She looked a lot younger than her years and made him feel much older than his. She turned her oval face towards him as he unloaded a long, rakish Colt pistol, spilling the bright brass loads onto the Indian rug that covered the bed, then worked the weapon's action, looking critically at it. The scabbard for the Colt was worn on the man's left hip, and when he was wearing his knee-length coat, was not visible.

She said, 'I'd not look forward to crossing those hills.' He would have known that. But if it turned out to be what they had to do she would not keep complaining about it. He said, 'Or we could head north from here, more towards Shelby. As long as we by-pass Shelby itself. Or we could cut norwest, down Loretta Creek way, lose him in all that brush country down there an' come out finally in Marietta County.'

She thought about that, then asked, 'Wouldn't that mean we'd have to cross Warren County? Some part of it?'

Strickland was reloading the Colt, thumbing the fat bullets in, concentrating, not looking at her. 'Yeah, I know it. But the way I figure it, what it comes down to, it's that or take on the Tessora Hills. To me, Marietta County looks to be the easier way.' He slid the Colt away.

To her chagrin she found herself pitying him. Suddenly she wondered if the Warren County sheriff's office was displaying the dodger with his face on it. $8,000. Dead or alive. She continued to marvel at the fact that there were men he still trusted, those in Helena, others in other places who, he said, *went back a long way.* For that kind of money she marvelled that none of them had turned him in long since. Might do it though, still? She shuddered and he noticed and left off examining the Winchester he had picked up.

He tossed the rifle on the bed and came to her.

'Stel, I'm real sorry. For the way it's turned out.'

'It's not your fault. None of it's your doing. It's this ... *leech*.' Then, 'How long do we have?'

One arm resting across her straight, narrow shoulders, he too staring down onto the dismal street, he shrugged. 'Two, three days. I can't be sure. Maybe not as long as that.' Maybe not nearly as long was what he was thinking.

She said, 'I shouldn't have harped on about stoppin' here.'

He shook his head. 'It's all right. It's fine. You can only take so much.'

She sighed and rested her dark head against his chest. 'So. Across a small bit of Warren County. That's what it's to be?'

'Unless I've got it worked out all wrong, we'll still have time to git across Warren County an' be inside Marietta County well ahead o' this bastard. If he knows anything about me at all then he never would pick me to risk crossin' Warren County. Nobody that knowed me would expect that. An' he'll have been askin' his questions.' By now Stone would indeed know plenty. For example, he would know about *her*.

'I hope you're right.' She stayed near the window as he moved away and went across and picked up the rifle again, hefting it, sighting it, stroking a hand against the brass frame. When he was handling weapons there was always an economy of movement and, as always, it sent a chill through her. In one silent stride he was a long way from the dirt farmer that he had become. She watched as he propped the Winchester in a corner of the room.

He said, 'Let's go eat.'

Later, lying alongside him, she found that, tired as she was, she was unable to slip easily into sleep. Every sound in the near-empty hotel seemed magnified. Ominous. Already she was in the power of the unseen and unexpected Rudolph Stone, a man who could reach out across this wild country to touch the likes even of Jack Strickland and send him bolting for cover. It sent a fresh shudder through her, but this time Strickland did not notice and come to her, for he was breathing evenly, in sleep.

Next morning they were on the trail early, before the night's chill had properly lifted off the land, on walking horses, trailing their laden pack-animals, heading out of Dorelia. Now Stella was reflecting on the great number of departures there seemed to have been during their life together. The narrow, slightly hunched figure up ahead of her was that of a man isolated from her, trapped in his own thoughts. He would be hating this. Running. *Dragging her with him* would be how he would see it, though she had come willingly enough. Other thoughts intruded, because only a few miles ahead of them lay a toe of country that was a part of Warren County. Those thoughts she had to make a conscious effort to thrust aside.

As the day had worn on, their pauses had

been brief. Stella had begun to wonder if he intended making a camp at all, preferring, perhaps, not to break the insistent rhythm of the journey. But nearing sundown he drew his horse to a halt along with the pack-animal he was leading, and waited for her to come up with him. Across to their left, among scrappy brush, in country that was strewn with hardy vegetation of all kinds, was a large upthrust of greyish rock. Now walking his horses on again, Strickland headed towards it.

At first Stella thought that this was to be their campsite but watched in silence as he dismounted and walked stiffly to the great rock. He examined it, looking for hand-holds and places where he could fit the toes of his boots. Then, stepping up, seeking and testing, he climbed slowly until he was at the pinnacle of the rock. He lay there staring back the way they had come. Time passed. Minutes stretched into a quarter of an hour. Strickland then began descending, boots scraping, once slipping but recovering. On the ground, for the space of half a minute, he rested, gloved hands braced against his knees. When he looked up at her with his time- and strain-creased face, she could see that something was wrong.

'What is it?'

'Mile or so back. Somebody. One man. There an' then not there. But gittin' closer. Headin' right this way.'

She drew a quick breath. 'Jack, it can't be!'

'It can be. It might. I coulda got the timin' worked out all wrong. Can't afford to think it couldn't be him.'

She felt cold, knowing that he believed it was Stone. The light was going but there was still plenty to see by. And to be seen. Strickland told her that she must take charge of both the packhorses and lead them deep in among the tallest brush nearby. 'Try to find some place where it ain't easy fer somebody to git behind yuh.'

She set about doing as he wanted, but asked, 'Where will you be?'

'Tryin' to watch this bastard all the way

in.' He cast a glance at the sky, then un-shipped the Winchester and held it out to her. Wordlessly, she took it. Strickland secured the lines from the pack-animals to Stella's saddle horn. 'Go. Now.'

He watched as she began moving away. Then he went back to the uplifted rock and again set about a careful, laborious ascent. By the time he reached the top he was breathing hard.

The light was now greyer. He could see no one on the move but believed he had heard the sound of a shod hoof striking against flinty stone. And not far away. He strained to hear more, but could not. A horse whickered but the sound had come from somewhere behind him. One of those with Stella. He turned his head but could not see where she was. Strickland went inching down, boots seeking out the toe-holds.

On the ground, standing in bunch-grass, he swept back the long coat and drew the rakish Colt. A slight breeze had risen, washing through the brush, just sound enough to mask other noises. Again a horse whickered. Strickland's face was deeply creased as he squinted through the gathering gloom, a poor quality of light that could turn more remote brush into images of men. His eyes ached from staring. He shut them hard, opened them again, and there he was. About sixty feet away, afoot, the faint glint of a pistol showing as it was moved.

'Jack Strickland?'

'It is.'

'Figured it was.'

'Yuh come up with me quickern I'd thought.'

'Yuh lit out from that there dirt farm quickern *I* thought.' Then, 'Where's the woman?'

'Gone. Long gone.'

'Yuh ain't much of a liar, Jack.'

Strickland said, 'From what I've heard, Rudy, I'd not have picked yuh fer a man to stand around palaverin'.' He thought he heard Stone laugh. Strickland moved at the same instant that Stone moved, side-stepping, pistol-arm lifting, then chopping down, blasting, both shooters flicker-lit. Then Stone was gone from sight. Not hit, so Strickland thought. Neither was he but he had felt the waft of heavy lead whipping by him, ripping through brush.

They began a shifting fight, appearing and suddenly shooting with startling brightness, just as suddenly vanishing, the breeze carrying the gunsmoke away and the acrid fumes of gunfire. Strickland paused, listening. Nothing. Then suddenly, Stone's hard voice came, calling, 'Stella ... I got Jack! Jack's shot!'

She heard it clearly, borne on the breeze. She began moving even as Strickland's yell came hard on the heels of Stone's words. 'Don't move, Stel! Bastard's playin' games!'

She could have sworn she heard laughter. Then there was another fierce eruption of gunfire, then a pause, then an isolated shot. Silence, then, but for the stirring of the brush all around her. She gripped Strickland's Winchester and began walking.

Six

Tom Strickland had gone the rounds knowing that probably he was knocking on dead doors, yet carrying out what he saw as the very least of his duties, trying to locate anyone at all who might have been witness to the events surrounding the raid on the Redrock County Jail. Resigned to failure and much dispirited, he had come back without one jot of useful information which might have helped him find out who the raiders had been.

And he had been out to the Rocking M ranch where, predictably, he had clashed with its testy boss, Nate Miller, a man who had, in fact, become near apoplectic when confronted by Strickland who had ridden in leading the strong saddler that had been used by one of the killers, one with the

Rocking M brand. Naturally, Miller strongly denied that he or any of his riders had been a party to the busting out and the subsequent deaths of the Doyles.

'You're getting to be real careless with these horses of yours,' Strickland said, a remark which served only to stoke Miller's temper the more. One or two of his ranch hands, working around a corral, paused to watch and to listen as their employer and the Warren County Sheriff stood almost toe to toe, voices raised, the one venting his different frustrations in the face of the other. This was, of course, the culmination of all the rawness that had arisen during the embittered progress of the Strickland posse. Eventually, Strickland had departed from the Rocking M but not before he had reminded Nate Miller that no doubt he would be summoned to appear in person at any subsequent enquiry, probably at a full inquest, to account for the presence of the Rocking M horse. Strickland had not waited around for a response.

In Redrock, the mayor, John Straker, came around to the county jail, pressing for answers: to the Doyle business which, as he said once again had unsettled the entire community: about the shooting of the drunk man *right out there on Front Street,* an act which had resulted in that unknown man's death.

Frederic Earl, the pale-faced doctor who had attended the man, was not saying much, and it would be the other doctor, George Halliburton, who would conduct the inquest.

'Inquests, inquests, inquests,' Straker said, the rounded man standing there in his ulster and his derby hat. 'All on a sudden it's all goddamn' inquests!' It was as though his politician's eye was visualizing streets littered with dead. And the whole thing was real bad for commerce.

'I'll be there,' said Strickland, 'to give my account of the circumstances.'

'An' there'll be a whole damn' string o' hard questions that'll want answers.'

'Then I'll just have to take 'em as they come.' Strickland was sick to death of the likes of Straker, particularly coming hard on the heels of the run-in with Nate Miller. And no sooner had Straker gone waddling out than Jasper Fox came by. It was he who, seeking to find out when the inquests might be held – for no doubt he saw himself as being involved, at least in the bringing in of the Doyles – dared to give voice to the name of Jack Strickland.

'I know it's a kinda touchy subject,' Fox said, softly, looking innocently bland in the face of Strickland's stony stare, 'but if you ain't heard yet, maybe you should.' When Strickland failed to respond, Fox, seemingly unfazed, went right on. 'One way an' another I get to hear all kinds of talk. Freighters comin' an' goin'. Railroad people. The word I keep hearin' is that brother o' yours, he's got some bountyman on his trail.'

For the space of a few seconds, Strickland considered taking hold of Fox by the front of his well-cut coat, but with an effort overcame that impulse. Instead, his voice steady, Strickland asked, 'Is there more?'

Head held slightly on one side, Fox pursed his thin lips. 'Strickland, you know as well I do that rumours kinda blow around on every shift o' the wind. But there was a name I heard that kinda made me listen to this one.'

'What name?'

Fox paused, maybe choosing to draw it out for greater effect. 'Rudolph Stone.'

Strickland's expression remained impassive but the name had come with the impact of a bullet. The earlier faint, elusive rumours about where Jack might be or might have been seen, were nothing new. From time to time all kinds of hints and whispers did circulate; and some, so Strickland suspected, might well have been manufactured maliciously, with the deliberate purpose of unsettling him. Indeed it had been a succession of rumours, as well as the roughness of life here, that finally had led to the break between him and Grace. Yet through all of that, and before and since, he had contrived to remain outwardly unmoved, unprovoked. Now, however, and coming as it did from the last man in Warren County he would have wished to hear it from, this was something that had a firmer ring to it. Stone's was not a name to be taken lightly.

Yet to Fox he said, 'Saying a name's easy enough. Stone's or any other.'

Fox, smiling in the irritating way that sometimes he affected, merely shrugged, his whole attitude seeming to say, *Suit yourself. I came here in good faith.* Fox nodded and left. Strickland stood watching him going pacing across the street and along the boardwalk on the further side where, apparently by chance, he stopped to speak with Besant and Faulkner as they emerged from a saloon. The three fell into a quiet conversation but not before Fox had taken a cautious look over his shoulder as though to ensure that they were not being overheard. Then he began talking earnestly, clearly dominating what was being said, using hand gestures to override interruptions, and manifestly displeased about something. When Fox had finished what had plainly been a harangue he walked off and left the pair of them to go shambling away. It was obvious that both of them had been at the bottle.

The deputies came in. Harry Neal's head was still heavily bandaged and he was looking very seedy indeed. Jase Lowell, florid and seemingly disquieted about something – not an unusual condition for Lowell – Strickland got the impression that neither of them were anxious to meet his eye. Strickland reached his hat off its peg and went out. Perhaps they had been sounded out by various parties over the tale that Jasper Fox had been carrying.

Outside, in the distance, beyond numerous people moving along the boardwalk, he glimpsed Fox himself walking now with Brodie Culp, just stepping inside Culp's saloon. It occurred to Strickland that, if Culp did not yet know of the Rudolph

Stone rumour, he soon would do, and from that point on, all of Redrock would know it. Indeed, soon enough there came to Strickland the feeling that the story had already gained plenty of currency, probably through the same people who had brought it to Jasper Fox, for as Strickland moved around through the town he was being looked at with particular interest. Once, long ago, Jack had said, I *never will throw a shadow anywhere near yuh.* And a clear image of that hard, unschooled man who was his brother, came to him. As always it bothered him, yet there was a warmth there still, and always, the reality of kinship. Then, too, there were things that Tom knew that others could not know. But he had never sought to excuse what had happened, the kind of life that Jack had chosen to lead in the wildness of his youth, riding with the wrong bunch, a prey to drink. Eventually, however, prison had put an abrupt end to that. An end to the risks, the foolishness, the belief that the worst things happened only to others, not to him, Jack Strickland. He had emerged from behind the grim walls of that place a vastly changed man. Tom had then and had now no doubts at all about that. A different man and a better man. The guilt of the past all washed away, Jack wanting only to live the quiet life, turn his back on that ugly past, still supported by the dark-haired woman who, resolutely, had stood by him all through. Until smoking blasts of gunfire on the main street of Torrega and the hurried ride out of the masked bandits had flung his name up once again.

At the ragged, weedy end of a blind street bounded on three sides by a corral and some storehouses, Strickland came to a halt. A quiet backwater. Slowly he began re-tracing his steps. He glanced skywards. Soon it would be sundown. After that he would begin his rounds of the streets as was his well-known custom, an unhurried progress, showing the badge, looking in at busy saloons, trying doorlatches at dark-ened buildings.

When the darkness did come down he sent Deputy Neal back to the Front Street rooming-house where he lived, leaving Jase Lowell in charge of the office, and went out again. His slow-pacing tour through the Redrock streets underscored his belief that he was being regarded with a certain wariness. Merchants with whom he was accustomed to passing a few words seemed suddenly busier than usual. Those he did speak with, however, were courteous. Carefully so? Deference to the office he held would be sufficient still for that. Many among them though, as he knew, would be anticipating the inquest which would be held over the death of the stranger who, drunk and aggressive as he had been, was perhaps no worse than many another who had been dealt with in the past. But this one had fallen to Strickland's pistol.

Strickland could not avoid the thought that there was under all this the influence of Jasper Fox. With Straker, Fox would doubt-less be contending that such violence was bad for Redrock. Bad for business there. It was hard to argue against that. Yet there was a certain hypocrisy, too, for it was really all to do with politics. Which brought him right back to Jasper Fox and to that man's close friend and business associate, Brodie Culp. Under the name of Redrock Enterprises, those two owned numerous premises and as yet undeveloped land around town and well outside it.

Strickland, because he always took an interest in the less lighted places now arrived in such an area behind some buildings and where there were several unkempt lots. Strickland turned then and slowly made his way towards an alley that ran alongside the Criterion Hotel. Passing close to some small outbuildings, and in deep shadow, he heard his name spoken.

'Tom?'

Abruptly Strickland stopped. He turned his head, eyes straining to pierce the darkness. He had felt a stab of shock for he had no need to ask who it was whose outline he could now faintly see. In a low voice he said her name.

'Stella....' She was still hanging back in the shadows, so he went to her. Her face was only a pale wash in the night. She almost fell against him and he was aware of the shuddering tension within her. 'My God, Stella, what is it? What are you doing here? Where's Jack?'

'He's been shot ... Jack's been shot. There was a man ... come hunting him.'

The words drummed at Strickland, but he said, 'A marshal?'

'No. Some bountyman. A man Jack got to hear about, in Helena. Tom, it was unlike Jack to do what he did. It seemed to scare him real bad. Enough to have us pull out an' get away from where we were in a real hurry. The bountyman's called Rudolph Stone.' In the cold silence perhaps she felt his involuntary reaction. 'You know that name?'

'I do. What happened?'

'We ... thought we were in the clear. We weren't. Stone caught up with us. We'd not long crossed Loretta Creek, in thick brush country.'

'I know it.'

'Jack, he didn't want to come across the Warren County line, but in the finish he thought it was the quickest ... the safest way. We were going to head up towards Shelby.'

'So what happened?'

'When Jack saw a rider comin' he thought it was Stone. He sent me an' the two pack-horses we had into the brush, an' waited. There was a shoot. It went on for a while. They were movin' around. The light was just about all gone. Then Jack an' this Stone got closer an' there was a lot of shootin'. Stone's dead, but Jack was hit too. Badly. He took a ball in the left thigh. It's still in there, deep. I think maybe the bone's broken.' Her voice altered. 'Tom, he needs help. Proper help. More than I can give him.'

Strickland's thoughts were spinning fast. He was well aware of the dangers of such a wound. If it became infected, almost certainly gangrene would set in. Gas gangrene, leading to a hideous death, in dreadful pain. But *proper help* meant a doctor. A doctor surely meant the discovery of Jack Strickland as a wanted man. $8,000, dead or alive.

'Where is he? Still 'way out there?'

'He is. I tried real hard to help get him up in the saddle, but Tom, it was hopeless. For a while, he passed right out. Somebody, a doctor ... a druggist, needs to be got out there.' She hesitated, then went on, 'I ... we didn't want to get you involved. But the closest town was Redrock. I knew there'd be risks to you as well as Jack.' Then, 'I made a fire. I left more dry brush within reach for him...' Her words faded away to nothing.

Strickland realized that she had been pushed to her limits. He was still very close to her, and then her paltry weight was leaning against him.

'You need to go somewhere to rest, Stella. You're not known here. Not as far as I know.'

'I'm never sure, Tom. You can't ever tell just who might be around. Who might remember a face. I can't take the risk of being recognized. If anybody did, they'd start wonderin' where Jack could be.'

Strickland stepped slightly away. She might well have divined the reason. If she did she would indeed have known why, acknowledged that once, in the past, they had come unexpectedly close, then in confusion, drawn instantly away. As he had done now. Even in this dire situation Strickland was astonished to find that something of that still remained, and was thankful for the cloaking darkness.

'I've got a place, a house, on the next street off Front Street. Only three other houses along there. I'll take you. You can rest up, out of sight. The horse you came on, where is it?'

'Hitched to a gate in back of the shack over there.'

'Somebody might notice an' wonder. I'll come back an' get him. Hide him away somewhere.'

'What can you do for Jack? Would the

doctor go out?'

'There's two in Redrock. The one I know better is Halliburton. But he's a strange man. Never know what Halliburton might do. I don't know, Stella. I can only try.'

'Maybe I should go talk with him. You stay clear of it. Tom, I'd do near anything to keep Jack out of their hands. He didn't have any part of what went on in Torrega that time.'

'Well, the men who saw the bandits heading out, an' reckoned they'd heard the name Jack, they're dead. I don't know why. They were busted out of my cage an' shot. Taken a couple of miles outside of Redrock. Seems to me somebody wanted 'em out of the way real bad.'

She sighed. 'Will you take me to this Doctor Halliburton?'

'It's a big risk for you. His surgery's along Front Street. He lives over it. Couldn't be more public. Maybe somebody *will* notice. An' Halliburton, he's the sort who asks a whole lot of questions.'

'As far as he's concerned, I'll be no more'n

some sodbuster's woman, come for help after an accident. Is there a back way we can use, at Halliburton's?'

'Yeah. But George is dead set on everybody using the front door. Day or night.'

She thought about it. 'There's another doctor?'

He nodded. 'Name of Fred Earl. But I can't see Earl going out. He's not a well man, not strong. No, it's got to be Halliburton.'

'Well, one way or another, I've got to get some help to Jack, an' soon.'

He could see that, weary though she must be, and afraid, she had a determination to see this through.

He said, 'I'll come out with you, to Jack.'

'No! He'd not want that. It's bad enough for him that it's come to this, in Warren County. As long as you were here he'd sworn he'd never set foot in it.'

'I'll take any chances there might be.' She stared at him and must have realized that there would be no arguing with him. They set off for George Halliburton's surgery Stella walking with her head down.

There were things that Strickland could not have known. One was that a man named Al Niebert had arrived in Redrock. The other was that, as she had feared, Stella Holman had been noticed while approaching Doc Halliburton's surgery, in the company of Tom Strickland. Word of it had not been long in reaching Jasper Fox and Brodie Culp, and it caused speculation.

'That wife o' his come back?' suggested Culp, who had always had an eye for Grace Strickland.

Fox did not give that a lot of thought, shaking his head. 'A dark-haired woman was what was said. Can't be Strickland's wife. And whoever she was she was in a ridin' outfit. Came in from somewhere.' Yet it was Strickland who, as a matter of course, was being watched. Seeing a woman with him had been unexpected.

Niebert was standing in the room too, a room in which all but one lamp had been turned down. A strange man, Niebert, tall, broad of shoulder but softly moving. He was dressed in dark-coloured cord pants, a blue shirt and a brown leather jacket with brass studs. The jacket was hanging open. His hat was grey, flat-crowned. Niebert's face was narrow with prominent bones and his eyes were like black beads, seeming never to blink. Snake's eyes.

Fox asked him, 'Anybody see yuh come in?'

Niebert shook his head, the merest of movements. He was a man manifestly more dangerous than even Besant or Faulkner. Their fault, as Fox was well aware, was that they were too often at the bottle to be wholly reliable. Well, they had been told that Niebert was coming and had had very little to say. But it had stopped even Besant in his tracks. Culp, surprisingly, had said of Niebert, *'Cold bastard.'* And he had taken a very thoughtful drink. But it was Culp's money as well as Fox's that had brought the man to Redrock *to lend a hand with one or two deals,* as Fox had put it. But now he said, 'First, there could be somethin' else that needs lookin' into here. Ever heard of Jack Strickland?'

Niebert nodded. 'Sure 'nough have. Still big money out fer Jack.'

Fox then told the black-eyed man what the present situation was. 'There's been a whisper here an' there about Jack.' The unmoving, black eyes were fastened on him. 'Brother Tom bein' seen here with a woman kinda raises somethin'. Took her to a doctor's door. Now, if she's who I think she could be, she could well lead a man right to Jack Strickland. Mebbe Jack's been hurt.'

Softly Brodie Culp said, 'Eight thousand dollars. One o' them that was shot that time, in Torrega, was a government man, so it turned out.'

To Niebert, Fox said, 'Ol' Jack could turn out to be a real bonus. Dead or alive.'

A slight flicker of the dead, dark eyes was likely the nearest indication of emotion that Niebert was ever likely to show.

Seven

After Doc Halliburton, in shirtsleeves, had opened the Front Street door of his surgery, Strickland did not go inside with Stella, content merely to see her admitted. But not before Halliburton had given him a probing stare and the briefest of nods.

To Stella's back, Strickland said, 'I'll be back.' That was as much for the doctor's benefit as hers. Strickland wondered if he had not been standing at the door with her whether George Halliburton would have let her in at all.

Inside the county sheriff's office, Deputy Lowell, scowling over paperwork, a task never to his liking, raised his thick eyebrows when Strickland came in and said, 'Jase, I'm gonna be out of town for a few hours. It's something that can't wait.' Then, 'You talked with Harry yet?'

'That I did,' said Lowell, staring at Strickland and clearly hoping for further enlightenment; but when it was plain that it was not to be forthcoming, he added, 'Reckons he'll be along soon. Haid's still hurtin' him real bad, but he claims he kin put in time here better'n where he's at.' Knowing the spartan conditions in which Deputy Neal lived, Strickland evinced no surprise at that. Then he crossed to the gun rack and took down his Winchester. He then left the yellow-lit office, walking out and around the long building and across a yard to a stable at the rear. By lantern-light he blanketed and saddled his bay horse. He secured a bedroll as well. He extinguished the lantern and led the horse out and around some neighbouring backstreets to the secluded place where Stella's horse was tied. When, soon, he emerged, mounted on his own animal, he was leading Stella's horse.

In Halliburton's rooms, the doctor, though he had put a heavy jacket on and had checked his bag, was still far from content. The small woman he had admitted, a woman dressed in a divided skirt and a thick coat with a thrown-back hood and of an age he put at late thirties, certainly appeared to be under some stress. Her delicate oval face was framed by very dark hair that was secured in a thick bunch at the back of her neck. Her obvious good looks were spoiled somewhat by tensions and by what clearly was lack of sleep in recent times. Her tale of her sodbuster husband had sounded persuasive; yet something was telling Halliburton that there was an untrue ring to it that he could not identify. In the finish, however, his professional duty had prevailed and now he snapped his bag shut and nodded. After all he had no good reason to disbelieve her. And she had gone first to the county sheriff.

'I've got a buggy but I'll not take it. From what you've told me about where he is, there's too high a risk of damage to it. I'll go saddle a horse. Did I understand Sheriff

Strickland to say he'd be back?'

'He seems set on comin' out there.'

Halliburton grunted, staring at her. She
sure looked done in. Then he said, 'Ten
minutes. Wait out front.' A blunt man by
nature, his abruptness of manner caused
Stella to blink, but she remained close-
mouthed and lowered her eyes. Halliburton
walked through with her and opened the
front door, letting her out onto the boardwalk. She heard him sliding bolts. Nearby
there was a lantern on a pole. She pulled her
hood up. There were some movements up
and down the street, people about, but it
was the mounted man on a walking horse
and leading another that grabbed her attention. Tom Strickland. A mixture of relief and
something else welled up in her. She drew in
a long, somewhat unsteady breath.

Not much more than ten minutes later all
three were heading out of Redrock. Halliburton was clad now in a long leather coat
and a narrow-brimmed hat and with his
medical bag slung at his knee, secured by a

thong around the saddlehorn. Stella led out, followed by Halliburton, Strickland riding some five yards behind the doctor. Soon the lights of Redrock fell away behind them. The chill of the night struck at them and Strickland pulled up the collar of his jacket.

Presently they came to the night-glitter of the Slee River and began following it south westward. This was taking them into rougher country with much brush and numerous up-crops of rock. No sodbusters hereabouts. All of them were scattered along the more northern reaches of this river. If Halliburton had been thinking about where this particular sodbuster and his wife had come from and where they might have been heading, he did not pursue the matter. Certainly Halliburton seemed to want to ride on his own, hunched down in the saddle, content merely to follow the indistinct shape of the woman riding half-a-dozen yards ahead of him. Halliburton was in fact more unsettled of mind than he had been when she and Tom Strickland had come knocking at his surgery door. While saddling his horse and securing the bag, the doctor had formed the distinct impression that there was someone else quite nearby in the cloaking darkness. He had even walked across the small yard carrying his lantern asking, *'Who's there?'* But there had been no answer much less any sight of another presence.

In Redrock, Deputy Harold Neal, still feeling very unwell, had come down the un-covered stairs of the cold rooming-house and had paused in the doorway, quietly observing the street but without particular interest. In a minute or two he would head on down to the county office. Now, how-ever, his attention was caught by a woman partly lit by lantern-light, outside Doc Halliburton's. Tom Strickland was there, too, mounted and leading another horse. The woman got up in the saddle and almost at once Doc Halliburton, on a walking horse, came out of an alley, and joined Tom and the woman. All three went riding up the main street, clearly heading out of town.

What emergency might have occurred sufficient to take not only Doc Halliburton away at such an hour, but Tom Strickland as well, young Neal could not imagine. Maybe Jase Lowell would know. About to move on out, Neal hesitated. No more than a couple of doors along to his left he noticed Tex Faulkner and Jake Besant who had emerged from the Cattlemen's saloon, somebody else standing there in the doorway, somebody Neal couldn't see – Culp, perhaps – and there was a man next to Besant who was a stranger. Lamplight from the saloon played across the stranger's face. There was something about the set of him that caused Neal to take notice. Dark pants, high-collared leather jacket with brass studs, flat-crowned grey hat. But it was not the clothing that was making Neal stare. It was some strange aspect to the man that Neal could not rightly identify; but whatever it was it gave the deputy an uncomfortable feeling. Presently Faulkner and Besant went inside the saloon. The stranger did not go in with them. He went to a hitched horse at the tie rail, a strong-looking black, and mounted up. Neal watched as he went by, heading away up the main street in the same direction as that taken by Strickland, Doc Halliburton and the unknown woman. Coincidence? Thoughtfully, Neal moved right out of his doorway and walked away towards the county jail. The night was chilly and his head was aching very badly, and now he regretted having told Jase Lowell that he would put in an appearance at all tonight.

When, however, he did arrive at the office, he passed on to the dour older man what he had noticed along Front Street. But thinking that Lowell might be dismissive, as so often was the case, he added, 'Could be somethin' an' nothin'.'

Lowell was now ready to go out on an unhurried tour of Redrock which he knew Strickland would expect, *business as usual,* showing the badge. And it was in Lowell's nature, when Strickland was absent, to show his authority as well, let all and sundry know that, for the time being at least, he was the man in charge.

To Neal he said, 'Tom come in an' told me he was headin' out o' town. Didn't say why an' didn't say where. What he did say was it warn't fer long.' Lowell scratched slowly at his ribs. 'A woman, yuh say?'

Neal nodded. 'Seen her in the light by Doc Halliburton's. Dark-haired woman, I reckon. Got a look at her afore she pulled a hood up. Halliburton, he come ridin' his hoss from out o' the alley, an' as soon as he come they all of 'em rid out. Never see'd that woman afore.'

Lowell, not having witnessed this departure, asked, 'Which way they headed?'

'Aw, I'd reckon towards the Slee.' And he added, 'Not wastin' no time about it, neither.'

'Gawd alone knows why Tom would wanta go with 'em,' Lowell said. Then, 'This other feller, the one that was with Faulkner an' Besant, yuh sure yuh ain't seen 'im afore?'

'Never clapped eyes on the *hombre*,' Neal said. 'But I'd say he warn't no cowhand nor no sodbuster nor no drummer. Reckon Culp was standin' there an' all, in the door at the Cattlemen's. Tex, he was out on the boardwalk an' so was Jake. Soon as they went back in, that feller got mounted an' he headed out the same way as Tom an' them. An' he warn't wastin' no time neither.'

Lowell thought it over. Though he did not say so to Harry Neal he reckoned that if the opportunity came, he might just have a word with Faulkner or Besant, if only to let them know that the county law seldom took its eye off them. The sending of such messages, so Lowell firmly believed, went a long way towards keeping a lid on the town's tougher element.

Well away from Redrock now, riding through the barely moonlit night, the silver snake of the Slee, glimpsed between trees and ragged brush, now across to their right, Stella Holman, George Halliburton and

Tom Strickland were travelling as quickly as they prudently could. Strickland was still trailing but Halliburton had just urged his horse forward to come up alongside the hooded woman.

'How far now?'

Strickland could not hear what her answer was, but whatever it was, Halliburton fell back again. Hereabouts the going was not easy, the ground dipping and lifting, the way ahead often impeded by looming brush that had to be avoided, the riders sometimes compelled to slow their horses almost to a walk. At one point Strickland took the opportunity to come to a brief halt. The horse stood blowing and shaking its head. For some time Strickland had had the uneasy feeling that someone else was abroad, and somewhere behind them. For almost a minute he sat listening, but he could hear nothing other than the shirring of the slight breeze through the brush. He hauled the horse around and set out after Halliburton and Stella Holman.

Halliburton, it seemed, had not even realized that Strickland had fallen back until he came up behind him again. But Stella knew. She fell back a little, but did not call him by name.

'What is it?'

'Maybe nothing. But we'd best go careful.' And for Halliburton's benefit, 'There's all sorts of men on the move, any time, after sundown. Warren County's no different to any other place, even if John Straker likes to claim it is.'

Halliburton grunted. It was impossible to know what his views were. More than likely he had begun to feel cramped and would certainly be cold, leather coat or not. Thus it was no doubt some relief to him when Stella said, 'There...'

Far ahead, sometimes obscured, reappearing, disappearing, a pinpoint of light in the velvet darkness.

In Redrock, Harry Neal, having had almost immediately to go around to the outhouse to vomit, had fallen prey to another pounding headache and had to go back to his rooming-house. Thereupon, not to set aside his patrol of the streets, Deputy Lowell locked the office and set out. In deference to the hour, activity had thinned out, though the saloons were still aglow as were some freight depots and one or two stores along Front Street. And the DeLange Hotel, down at the railroad end, where the whores were, was showing numerous lights.

Those who were still abroad tended, if they could, to avoid the path of the passing deputy, his thickset shape and swagger able to be identified, even on streets that were lit only poorly. A man of uncertain temper, Jase Lowell, apt to be intolerant, even dangerous. And if it was known that he – albeit temporarily – was the man in charge in Tom Strickland's absence, all the more reason to keep out of his way.

It was not too surprising, therefore, that no one else happened to be nearby when he came upon Faulkner and Besant in the act of shambling from one saloon to another. They were not so liquored up that they failed to recognize the man with the badge who had come to a spraddle-legged stop directly in their path.

Not bothering to mask his long-felt dislike of Besant in particular, for they had locked horns a time or two in the past, Lowell said, 'Didn't expect to find yuh still on the street at this hour, boys. Was I asked, I'da said yuh'd be in the DeLange by this, givin' a coupla li'l doves a tough time.'

'Wa-al, yuh woulda been blowin' your mouth out through your ass, as usual,' Besant said. 'Where I'm at an' what I'm doin' when I'm there ain't no bastard's business but mine, Lowell.'

Faulkner's right hand had lifted, thumb hooked in his belt close to the curved handle of his pistol. He was standing to the right of Besant and about a pace behind, belching softly, peering at the deputy with a slightly head-forward attitude.

'Yuh got some fancy notion o' pullin' that

thing?' Lowell asked. Faulkner, plenty of redeye aboard, possibly even weighing his chances, must then have reminded himself just who the man facing him was. Though he might indeed have fancied his chances of beating Lowell to it, here in a public place all hell would have broken loose if he had pulled a pistol on a county deputy. When Lowell realized that, if Faulkner had been on the brink, the moment had passed. To the pair of them he said bluntly, 'Some feller was in town earlier. Stranger. Hard man by his looks. Who was he? Where'd he come from?' He did not enlighten them as to who it was who had seen this man, leaving them to assume it had been him.

The nearer one, Besant, shrugged. 'Why ask us?'

'I'm askin' because it was you two that was jawin' with that feller,' Lowell said. It was plain to the deputy that his sudden questions had impacted on both of them, liquor-hazed though they were.

Besant said, 'Jes' some stranger, he was.

Passin' through. Didn't give no name an' we sure wasn't askin' fer one. Never see'd the feller afore an' don't reckon to ag'in. Wanted to know how far from Redrock to the Slee, an then which way to Helena.'

'Cattleman? Prospector? Surveyor? What?'

Faulkner had had enough of it and was still afire over being faced down. He came pushing forward. 'Goddamn it, Lowell! Jake, he jes' telled yuh we ain't never see'd the feller afore! If I'd wanted to know all them ins an' outs an' whichways, I'da gone an' got me a tin badge an' stuck it on my shirt long since!'

'Watch that mouth o' yourn,' Lowell said in a steady voice. He made a brief movement with his head. Dismissal. The talk was at an end. He did not move out of their way, however, so they needed to take care in easing on by him. Lowell knew full well that, a few paces beyond him, there would be resentful glances cast back at him. Lowell made a point of pacing on without looking around. He was feeling well satisfied, having put the two hardnoses off balance and having given the impression that there were things he knew that he was not letting on about. He had sown some seeds of uncertainty and felt well pleased about it. Nonetheless he now put them from his mind. He went on his way, soon leaving Front Street to cheek along numerous ill-lit or unlit backstreets. He passed by darkened buildings, barns, storehouses and a host of small outbuildings, some corrals and empty lots, railroad premises. Above and behind him the water-tower stood against a sky that was only lightened from time to time by a reap-hook moon. As he went, Lowell wondered some about Tom Strickland and what it might be that could possibly have taken him out of Redrock, at short notice, at night, in the company of Doc Halliburton and some woman. He spared thoughts also for Harry Neal in his present poor condition, and concluded broodingly that the young man was not going to be of much use to him in Strickland's absence, short though it was reckoned to be.

Lowell arrived at the junction of two backstreets and from where he was he could see the rear of the DeLange Hotel. For the space of a few seconds he considered visiting the place, then thought better of it and retraced his steps. He passed alongside the poles of a corral where there were a few horses. He headed for an alley that would bring him out on Front Street. What moon there had been was now completely obscured by cloud. All around lay deep shadows. He heard a voice, pitched low.

'Deppity?'

Something about it struck a chill into Lowell and he half turned towards where he thought the speaker was standing. Lowell's hand dropped to the handle of his pistol. At that instant two hammer blows sent him staggering, a pistol banging and flaring. It was so close that Lowell's shirt caught alight and in the flaring and the fire he glimpsed in the last moment of life the face of the man who had shot him.

Eight

Nearing the small camp that Stella herself had made, able to see the fire more distinctly now, they became aware, also, of the huddled, unmoving shape lying close to it. Before leaving she had laid out his bedroll and covered him with blankets, her own and his and the saddle blanket off his horse. The fire was burning brightly as though it had been fed not so long ago. Yet there was an inertness about the prone shape picked out by the flames sufficient for Stella to urge her horse forward more quickly. Halliburton, too, acknowledging urgency, followed her, then came Strickland.

Almost at the same time they dismounted, it was Strickland whose ear had caught the sharp, ratchety sound. He shouted, 'No, Jack! Hold up!'

129

In some confusion, Halliburton stopped and swivelled around and Stella did not bend to the blankets – for that was all that was there, made into a bolster – but straightened up slowly, turning, her eyes trying to pierce the darkness.

He was in among brush some twenty feet away, where he had managed to drag himself when he had first heard the horses coming, and he had the rakish old Colt pistol in his hand. Weak and in pain, somehow he had summoned the will to move himself away from the fire, dragging his badly injured leg.

Halliburton and Strickland went at once to take hold of the hurt man and, as gently as they could, bring him back to the spread of light from the fire so that Halliburton could get a look at the wound. To do it he had to take a knife and slit the leg of the man's pants. Throughout, Jack was gasping and grunting and at one point, cried out. Nonetheless Halliburton was soon able to say that the leg was not, as the woman had feared, broken. But he reckoned that the lead ball had hit and was lodged against the bone.

'That's what I think.' Then, as he opened his medical bag, looking quickly at Tom Strickland, said, 'I'll have to probe for it. It can't be left in there.'

Seeing a folded pad of cloth in the doctor's hand, the prone man then said, 'I ain't no ways gonna be doped out!'

'That's something you might well regret,' said Halliburton. And to Tom, 'You'll need to take hold of him, and firmly.' Then, 'Tom, I'm not a complete fool. I do know who he is, now. And you called him by his given name.'

Stella said, though not knowing where it might lead, 'Doctor, that was my doing. I thought ... maybe if you'd known, then you wouldn't have come...'

Searching around in his bag, the doctor said, 'Can't say what I'd have done. But I can say this: the sheriff of Warren County will soon have some hard questions to answer.' Having found the instruments he would need, he straightened. 'I'll want some more light.'

Strickland threw some more brush on the fire causing new flames to go leaping and sparks to fly up.

It took some ten minutes and a great deal of agony for the writhing man, biting on a wadded bandanna, Tom Strickland holding him, for the probing to produce the lump of lead. Halliburton himself, having laid aside his coat and rolled up the sleeves of his shirt, was sweating. Then he had to probe again, and this time removed a sliver of bone. Halliburton then cleaned and dressed the wound. But long before this, Jack Strickland had lost a good deal of blood, and the doctor also observed that the man's general physical condition had not been good. The doctor was plainly concerned about it. Stella used water from a canteen to dampen a cloth and with it gently wiped Jack's sweat-greasy face and neck.

Strickland asked, 'Where's the man who

did this?' When Stella told him he sought out the body. Presently he came back into the firelight.

'I'll pack Stone back into Redrock when we pull out of here.'

Halliburton said, 'That might not be for a while. Not 'til daylight, anyway. This man is in very poor shape. He'll need constant watching. He'll need to be kept warm.' But the doctor was still feeling most aggrieved over the deceit that had been practised upon him and that Tom Strickland, no less, had been a party to it. 'This man is wanted. Here he is, within your jurisdiction. No matter what your kinship is, you've got a duty to carry out, a professional duty, just as I have.'

'An' I don't have any answer,' Strickland admitted, 'except that I've never believed Jack had anything to do with what happened in Torrega. No matter what the Doyles said.'

'Those unhappy men are no longer alive to say anything,' said Halliburton. But for the first time his tone was not as confident, as though he was now connecting with Strickland's unspoken suggestion that, of all witnesses, the Doyles had been the least reliable. Something was disturbing the doctor. Yet Halliburton, albeit more quietly, said, 'Whatever you might want to believe, the reward was posted, the dodgers were circulated, and no matter how long ago it happened, nor who this man happens to be to you, the proper form to debate all that is a court of law.'

Stella, still attending Jack Strickland, half turned her head. 'He's drifting off some-times.' She pulled the blankets higher up under the prone man's chin.

Halliburton examined Jack again. Stella had stood up, moving back. Tom Strickland was now standing quite still, listening. From somewhere out in the darkness came the sound of a horse blowing. Strickland's right hand had scarcely moved towards the handle of his pistol when Niebert's hard voice came to them.

'Don't try fer it, mister!' There was the distinct sound of a pistol being cocked.

Strickland called, 'Who is it?'

'The man that's come fer the bastard yuh're all jawin' about.' There was no telling just how long this unknown man had been out there in the dark, in the quiet of the night, listening to what they had been saying. And in his near anger, Halliburton's voice had sometimes been raised.

Unexpectedly Jack Strickland's husky, gasping whisper came. 'Goddamn ... bountyman!'

The voice from beyond the firelight warned, 'Nobody but the badgeman move. You ... lift them han's up, away from the pistol.'

Quite slowly, Strickland did. When Stella Holman made as though to go to Jack who was obviously in great discomfort, she was told sharply to stand still. 'You an' all, Sawbones.' Halliburton's mouth was open, no doubt about to protest. He shut it. The punching manner of the words told him clearly that there would be no compromise.

Now the man who had been speaking came into the spread of the fire's light. A tall, somewhat angular man, bony-faced, wearing a flat-crowned grey hat, dark pants and a brown leather, brass-studded jacket. He was holding a long pistol. When he got closer to them it could be seen that his eyes were small and unwinking, like black beads.

Strickland had never seen this man before but knew as soon as he got a good look at him that he was not to be taken cheaply. The man holding the cocked pistol came forward, moving with uncanny stealth, much as an Indian would move. He reached for and took Strickland's pistol and tossed this into the brush. Easing around Strickland, he then stooped over the prone, blanket-covered man and demanded his pistol. This one he flung away as well, then backed off slowly, watching all of them.

He said, 'Got me a problem here. The on'y man I want is Jack Strickland.'

Halliburton could be still no longer. 'This

man can't be moved. Not yet.'

The pistolman, long barrel glinting in the light of the fire, with his other gloved hand stroked at his angular jaw. Though his broad-brimmed hat cast a shadow across his face, his eyes still glittered as he gave an impression that he was thinking over what Halliburton had said. Strickland, however, was thinking with a growing dread that this man had already made his mind up. Indeed, Strickland's worst fears were soon confirmed.

'Wa-al, Doc, seems to me there's but one way out o' this. Yuh reckon he's too bad to be moved. What I'm tellin' yuh is, I've come fer the bastard, an' now I kin tell yuh that's what I'm gonna do. Dodgers all say daid or alive. Which way it is don't make no odds to me.'

Stella started to say, 'You can't—'

'Stand still!' The words seemed to cut her like a whip.

Then to Strickland the pistolman said, 'Sure is a goddamn' funny ol' world, Sheriff.

Law says I oughta hand the man over to you. Now, there's a thing. Here yuh stand an' here he is. But I reckon it don't work that way 'twixt you an' him. So I cain't no ways deliver ol' Jack to yuh. Nope. Gotta find me some lawman that ain't no kin o' his'n.' Suddenly he extended his pistol-arm and centred the long barrel on Jack Strickland.

Now there was no holding Stella Holman. She bolted forward, holding out one arm as though to prevent what was about to happen. 'No-o!'

The flash of the pistol was bright and the weapon bucked in the hand of the shooter and the woman was hit solidly, a spray of blood flying as she crossed into the line of fire. Halliburton was shouting, Strickland stood aghast as Stella was flung down, falling across the blanketed man then rolling into the shadows.

The black-eyed man was standing now in a crouch, his arm coming down again, about to kill the man on the ground. A shot lashed, and in the act of aiming, Niebert was slammed hard and sent back-stepping in an odd, bandy-legged way, pistol arm swinging wide of his body. The pistol dropped from his hand and the man himself pitched backwards to the ground.

Jack Strickland had shot him, having been virtually lying on the Winchester, but he now slumped back, gasping. By some supreme effort of will, or more likely fury, he had fired the rifle one-handed.

Halliburton moved very quickly to where Stella Holman lay. Just as quickly Strickland crossed to where the pistolman had fallen, to make sure he was not about to get up. It took only seconds to confirm that the man would never move again. It took Doc Halliburton no longer to conclude that Stella Holman would move no more, either.

Maybe it was this appalling truth that triggered something in Halliburton, caused him to alter abruptly his position in this entire affair.

'Tom, this whole county has started to go mad. She's dead, this poor woman. Given no chance. Just shot down. He could have held off, not fired. He could have!' Halliburton had begun striding back and forth, shaken, appalled. 'And we all could have been murdered!'

'That one's dead, too,' said Strickland.

Halliburton said dolorously, 'Him. Out there, the one who shot your brother; this woman; the Doyles, father and son...' For some reason he did not say, *And the other one, the one shot by you in the main street of Redrock.* What the doctor did say now, however, was something which only in such dire circumstances, he would ever have con-tem-plated. 'Before the elder of the Doyles died, he was trying to say something to me. I couldn't understand much of it. It was very faint and quite, er, disjointed. But it did seem to be to do with that affair in Torrega.' Halliburton had ceased moving and now stared at Strickland, who came closer to the doctor.

'Did he say a name? Any name?'

'No. No, I can't say that. But I can tell you

he was most agitated. He was certainly making an attempt to say something. To tell me something. I'm convinced of it.'

More loudly than he had intended, Strickland said, 'You've said nothing about this 'til now.'

'Because there was nothing certain to say.'

'You're not only a doctor, you're the coroner in Warren County.'

'And as such I have to deal in evidence. I deal in facts. And first, I remind you that indeed I am a doctor. A professional man.'

Strickland turned away, disappointed and no doubt showing it. He knew he had been grasping at what was probably a non-existent straw. Halliburton had already turned and was again kneeling beside Jack who was breathing roughly. Strickland disconsolately walked across to look at Stella Holman's body. The left side of her head was a darkly bloodied mess. Strickland moved off into the brush and spent the next twenty minutes locating his pistol and Jack's.

In the first light of day a swamper outside a saloon dropped his steaming mop. Coming along Front Street was Tom Strickland on a walking horse, leading two others. One was carrying the bodies of two men the other the body of a woman. By the time Strickland arrived at the tie rail outside the county office people were coming out on the street. Soon a small crowd had gathered. An unshaven, haggard-looking Mayor Straker was there, his round face ashen.

Deputy Neal, looking pastily sick, came along the boardwalk, staring at the dead that Strickland had brought in. But his own news overrode even that. 'Tom, Jase Lowell's been shot, last night. He's daid.'

'Who did it?'

Neal licked dry lips. 'Nobody saw nothin'. Out on the rounds. He was seen on Front Street.'

'That's right enough.' As Strickland swung down, Jake Besant arrived. 'Me an' Tex, we talked with Jase some. Said he was lookin' fer some feller that had been in town askin' questions, like how to git to Helena.'

Strickland's hard eyes pinned Besant. 'Reckon he wasn't going that far. Maybe that's the man there, across that horse. The one keepin' him company is a man called Rudolph Stone.'

Straker managed to say, 'Sheriff we need a lot of answers as to what the hell's goin' on in this county!'

Jasper Fox came strolling along. 'We sure do, Tom.' A tautness about the man today, not quite as self-assured, staring at dead men. 'I heard Doc Halliburton rode out with you last night, and with a woman. Where's Halliburton?'

'He'll be back when he can. The woman, she's there on that horse.'

Almost yapping, Straker asked, 'Who is she, that woman?' Still aware that the link between Stella Holman and Jack Strickland must have been made already, Strickland did not reply, but Straker pushed on with it. 'Your brother's woman, by any chance? That right?'

When there was still no answer. Fox asked, 'Where is he, Strickland? Where's Jack?'

'Not anywhere near Redrock.' He could see that a complete denial would be useless. He had had no alternative to fetching the bodies into Redrock for decent burial, but as he had feared, it had now put him in a corner.

Straker, no doubt certain that he would now have solid support, said bluntly, 'Strickland, I don't see how it's possible for you to carry on bein' in office in this county. Seems to folks here that you're shelterin' a felon. A wanted man with a price on his head.'

Angrily, Strickland said, 'Somebody here sent that dead one right there out after us. After me, Halliburton an' that poor woman. A bountyman.'

Belatedly, Deputy Neal spoke up. 'This is him, the one I seen.'

Besant looked at him sharply, as did Faulkner, who had also arrived. Smoothly, Fox put in, 'I don't reckon anybody in

144

Redrock sent that man. Jake Besant said he was askin' direction, that's all.'

Strickland did not for an instant believe it but knew that arguing would be useless.

Straker said, 'Strickland, I got to demand that yuh stand down. Well, at least 'til this whole damn' mess is cleared up.' That Strickland held an elected office which outweighed Mayor Straker's mere civic authority, seemed of no account now. Straker must have known full well that the body of public opinion would be with him in this. His politician's nose would have sniffed it. The very muttering of the crowd seemed to support it. A lot of talk ensued, even some shouting. Brodie Culp had come and was talking with Fox and Straker. Yet beyond the crowd, on an old wagon, sat a sodbuster from the north-western reaches of the Slee, and his wife; a sad-looking pair, listening, not joining in the general, noisy scene. For the space of a few seconds, however. Strickland thought the man was indeed about to say something. In the finish, and though his wife seemed plainly to be urging him to do so, did not. He flicked the long reins and walked his team on. Strickland saw, too, that Tex Faulkner at least, had noticed the sodbuster's departure.

Still confronted by a now confident Straker, Strickland thought, *The hell with it.* He unpinned his badge and handed it to Straker. Seeing this, Deputy Neal looked as though suddenly he felt very much alone and uncertain. Somebody – Fox maybe – made a remark about appointing a town marshal. Straker picked up that notion very quickly and there followed a ragged discussion about it. Strickland had had enough. He untied the horses and walked away, leading them in the direction of an undertaker's premises. When he heard the cry for a posse to be got up, however, he stopped briefly. There was, it had become clear, an enthusiasm for hunting Jack Strickland down.

Nine

After the crowd had drifted away it had been Harry Neal who had come seeking Strickland, and to do it had hung around the untidy yard in back of Lacey's the undertaker's. Now, as the sole county law, Harold Edward Neal, still unwell, was also of most uncertain mind. He was a young man who had had grave responsibility thrust on him and was riven with self-doubt. Strickland, observing the deputy through one of the grimy rear windows, came outside, and he was looking grim.

'I've just been taking a look at old Jase Lowell's body. Whoever did it was standing so close his shirt caught alight.'

Hopelessly, Neal asked, 'Tom, who in the name o' God woulda done it?'

His mind much engaged by that same

question, Strickland said, 'It wouldn't have been a matter of a few crossed words. It had to be somebody he'd thrown some kind of scare into.'

'Couldn't have been that there feller that follered yuh out o' town,' Neal said.

Strickland shook his head. 'Jake Besant said plain enough he'd talked with that man. Him an' Faulkner. I doubt Jake would be fly enough to say that, just to look clean. Fox would though. Or Brodie Culp.'

There was something more on Neal's mind. 'Tom, I'm gonna have to git this here posse up. But I ain't gonna ask yuh where the hell he is.'

'Understood,' said Strickland. He had some sympathy for young Neal. 'But listen, Harry, go careful. I hear they're pushin' for Culp to be town marshal.'

'They'll be pushin' fer Culp fer county sheriff soon enough,' Neal mumbled.

Strickland nodded, angry with himself now for having handed them that chance much sooner than it might have come. But now he said, 'There was a sodbuster couple on a wagon listening to all the hooha. Know 'em?'

'Yeah, I seen 'em,' Neal said. 'Fosters. Took over the Leary place a year back. Her pa's farm.'

Now Strickland recalled them and thought, ruefully, that he should have done so earlier. Now, however, he came back to the matter of the posse. 'Drag your feet a bit if you can, Harry, but don't lock horns with 'em over it.' Neal nodded, but still looked uncertain.

A short time after, having put food into saddlebags, Strickland went riding out of Redrock. And not so long after that Jasper Fox went looking for Deputy Harry Neal to find out when the hell he was going to gather up a posse. He seemed to be having some trouble locating Neal and was getting into something of a fit about it.

A couple of miles outside Redrock, Tom Strickland caught up with the sodbusters' slowmoving wagon. When he came riding up alongside, the brown-shirted driver hauled back on the reins and brought his team to a halt. The farmer gave Strickland only a thin-mouthed stare, but the man's wife looked more welcoming.

To her husband she said, 'Now's your chance, Ed.' It occurred to Strickland that this was a revival of the exchange that he thought had begun in Redrock.

'Chance went with the badge they took off'n 'im.'

'Try me,' said Strickland, steadying his sidescrewing horse.

Foster looked like a stubborn man. 'Got nothin' to say.'

His wife, a plain woman in dull clothing. would not be still. 'Mr Strickland, while yuh was the county sheriff we figured they dasn't push us too hard.'

Strickland said, 'I don't understand that.'

In spite of Ed Foster's dark glances the woman refused to be still. 'My pa run our farm, thirty mile out. On the Slee. When he died it come to me. Right back then we started gittin' offers. Every one fer about half o' what that land's worth.'

'Offers, who from?'

'That man Fox. Keeps comin' back. Last time he brung another feller.'

'Did you know him?'

'Yeah. Man called Besant. Seen 'im in Redrock.'

Foster said, 'Martha–'

But once started, she would not stop. 'Mr Strickland, he puts the fear o' God in me, that Besant.'

Knowing that he had lost the tussle, Foster now said, 'We ain't the on'y ones. Nearest neighbour, Lee Farrel, Ben Oldring an' all, they been visited reg'lar. Now yuh ain't there they'll come pushin' harder.'

And if Brodie Culp did eventually get to be county sheriff, thought Strickland, the pushing would get harder still. But he did not say so. He turned his horse, not back towards Redrock but in a more south-westerly direction, towards where Halli-burton and Jack were and hoping that he could get there before any Redrock posse.

Even as these thoughts were passing through Strickland's mind, that posse, an unhappy looking Harry Neal to lead it, was preparing to mount up. With the deputy would be Jasper Fox, Brodie Culp and five townsmen, these mainly of Culp's choosing. Faulkner and Besant had been yelled for by Culp in the lobby of the DeLange Hotel, but the posse was not about to wait around for them any longer. Culp had merely called out to Besant, in particular, the general direction that the posse planned to take. Then he had gone stamping out importantly to join it.

Tom Strickland came to the campsite where George Halliburton and Jack Strickland were. Jack was still in no great shape, although Halliburton seemed reasonably satisfied with his patient's present condition, in the circumstances. Tom Strickland was now almost as concerned for Halliburton as for his brother.

'You ought to leave here now, Doc. Pull out an' get well clear. You've done your part an' more. There's a posse being got up an' it can't be far behind me. I can't guarantee your safety. I don't carry the badge any more.' He explained to Halliburton what had transpired in Redrock.

Yet George Halliburton's deep shock and anger over the shooting of Stella Holman was plain to see. 'That was a wanton killing, Tom. It was a terrible thing to happen. I can tell you it's shaken me badly, and I've seen a lot of deaths in my time. Somebody sent that man, I'm convinced of it. And the more I think about what those Doyles claimed, the more I think it suspect. I'd go as far as to say I think they made a mistake.'

In a weak voice, Jack Strickland said, 'Nobody in the county ... is gonna go along with that, doc...'

'Four men,' Tom said. 'They reckon one was Travis Finney an' another was Chicken Charlie Abbott. They're both dead. No other names were ever talked about, except

Jack's. That won't change now. Best leave, Doc. Time's running out.'

Halliburton shook his head. 'Not until this man can be moved.'

So time went by, the Redrock doctor becoming uncommunicative and occasionally staring into space. He did some pacing up and down. Strickland was still at a loss to read Halliburton accurately, yet he had just been more forthcoming than Strickland had expected him to be; admitting to changed beliefs. They all settled down to wait, and time passed.

The doctor turned his head quickly, however, when Strickland said, 'They're comin'.'

Jack Strickland must have heard, too, and struggled to sit up, pistol gripped sweatily in his right hand. At the same time, horsemen came into view.

Harry Neal was leading them. Strickland's eyes searched for Faulkner and Besant but failed to find them. The posse was straggling to a halt some forty yards away. Neal, Fox,

Culp and about five townsmen. No weapons drawn. Neal now nudged his horse and approached on his own and stopped some ten yards from Tom Strickland. Neal looked very uncomfortable.

Strickland said quietly, 'Take it easy, Harry, an' say what you've come to say.'

Neal continued the theme he had begun in Redrock about Jack being a wanted man. 'I got to take 'im in.'

Strickland said, 'I know the bind you're in, but Jack's my kin. He's hurt bad an' I won't see him rough-handled. Any sign of that an' it'll all turn to shit real fast. You've got to stand firm behind that badge.'

'I'll do it, Tom.'

Yet with a heaviness in his belly, Strickland thought that Harry Neal was never going to be strong enough. The dodgers said dead or alive. Strickland could still hear the dead bountyman's voice. But now Fox was approaching, and Brodie Culp. They reined in one on either side of Deputy Neal.

Fox asked, 'What's all the palaver?'

'The deputy's been giving us the word,' Strickland said, 'because he's the man with the authority here.'

Today Fox's customary urbanity was not in evidence. 'Well, we all reckon you've jawed long enough. Deputy Neal, why don't yuh get the man on a horse an' let's get the hell out of here?'

Suddenly George Halliburton came pacing to them and stood between Strickland and the three mounted possemen. 'That man back there,' said Halliburton clearly, 'is my patient. I'll say when he can be moved, Mr Fox, nobody else.'

Fox, though regarding the doctor coldly, was taken aback, for Halliburton was a man of influence and what he said could not easily be brushed aside. Yet Fox would not be deflected. 'Doc, we understand your position, but the deputy's got a clear duty: Jack Strickland's wanted for murder.'

'I am perfectly aware of the allegations against Mr Strickland,' Halliburton said testily, 'but listen carefully. I shall take responsibility, fully. When I judge that he can ride without doing further damage to his leg, I shall deliver him to Redrock. If you want to wait, you'd best make a camp here.'

Harry Neal, perhaps heartened by George Halliburton's stand, jumped in. 'Good enough fer me, Doc.' Then he took everybody unawares by saying, 'That's it! We're headin' on back.' Fox, and Culp had to move their horses in a hurry as Neal turned his mount and headed away. And they had no option but, however reluctantly, to follow him. Maybe Harry Neal would suffer for what he had just done, before long.

A couple of miles on, having been riding behind Neal in prickly silence, Fox had reason to be doubly displeased when the posse met up with the tardy Faulkner and Besant. Curtly, Fox told them what had occurred, as the remainder of the posse rode on. Some three miles further on the posse, well strung out now, Neal riding well ahead of the rest, did not notice that neither Besant nor Faulkner were any longer of the party.

Ten

Led by the unusually assertive Harry Neal, the posse had gone bobbing away, but Tom Strickland was still uneasy. Several in the group had ridden out most reluctantly. Halliburton, after his firm stand taken in front of Jasper Fox and Brodie Culp, and after counselling Jack Strickland to rest as well as he was able, had become taciturn again and had even gone about gathering dry brush with which to feed the fire. Tom Strickland took the opportunity to lead the horses down to the river. Down there beyond a fringe of trees he glanced at the sky. Not long to go 'til sundown. He had begun to think that the turning away of the Redrock posse might have been too easy. Neither Fox nor Brodie Culp, but in particular Culp, would be inclined to allow the young Deputy Neal to rule the roost.

After a while Strickland led the horses up nearer to the campsite and picketed them. Then from his saddle-bags he brought out some of the food he had fetched, and a coffee pot and set about making a meal.

Supper over, bedrolls were spread and the fire was built up. An hour later, full dark having come down, Strickland was disturbed by a sound and tried to shake himself out of his drowsiness. But not quickly enough.

There were two of them. Mounted men, coming quickly, whitish masks covering their faces. Gunflashes lit them briefly as they went spurring through the outer shadows, there for only seconds before vanishing into the dark. Both Strickland and Halliburton, coming to their feet, took hold of the wounded man by the arms and hauled him away from the firelight and into the cover of brush.

To Halliburton, Strickland said, 'Stay here an' keep low!'

Strickland drew his pistol and went jogging away, angling to the left. The riders were coming back. Deliberately, Strickland fired a shot in their general direction, the flash splitting the dark, marking where the shooter was. He dived to the ground as answering fire came and he saw the horsemen. He had drawn their fire, as he wanted to do, away from where the other two were. Strickland shifted his position. Then suddenly he saw someone afoot and from fifty feet away a pistol flared, flicker-lighting the masked shooter. Heavy lead racketed through dry brush above Strickland's head. Strickland let go a bucking shot, then went rolling to one side. He thought he might have got a hit, but for a minute or two all went quiet. Then there was the sound of horses again and there was no doubt that they were going away. Strickland made his way back to where Halliburton and Jack Strickland were sheltering.

'A couple o' them goddamn' possemen?'

Jack suggested.

Tom said, 'Could be. But not with Harry Neal's say-so.' He helped Halliburton move Jack back nearer the fire. He did not think the riders would be back. 'I reckon I burned one of 'em. Got a quick look. He had on a dark, high-collar jacket. I've seen Faulkner wearing one like it.' Jack didn't know who Faulkner was, but Halliburton did.

'That man wasn't with the posse. Nor the other one, Besant.' Then, 'Tom, what's all this about?'

Strickland took his time before answering. 'Something that's been building up for a while. Power in the county. Possessions. Land. Farmers along the upper Slee, they're being pressured to sell. I've just found that out. I should've known about it.' That was nagging at Strickland's conscience.

'Pressure? Who from?'

'I'm told it's Jasper Fox. Lately he's had Jake Besant in tow.'

Halliburton was taken aback. It was clear that he had no idea of any link between Fox and the likes of Besant, or of Fox's predations. He sighed and shook his head but did not pursue the matter. What he did say was that the trouble over Strickland and the sheriff's badge had taken him by surprise. 'A needless act. At least until public opinion could have been properly tested.'

Strickland said, 'I reckon I've been seen as standing in their way. Fox, Culp, others maybe. It'll make things simpler for Fox if one of his friends can get to wear the county badge. I took a chance that didn't work out. I made a bad mistake.'

Jack Strickland said, 'Them Doyles was at the back of this goddamn' mess.'

Tom said, 'I reckon the Doyles just plain got it wrong. Maybe they did hear a name. Maybe the same as yours. But there were plenty around willing to take the jump from Jack to Strickland.'

'Give a dawg a bad name,' Jack muttered.

Then Halliburton, having been mulling over all that had been said, spoke up. 'Jack? Or Jake? Maybe that's the name the Doyles thought they heard.'

Tom said, 'It would explain a lot. But there's no evidence.' That would count with Halliburton, the man of facts, evidence. Due process. Yet perhaps Halliburton was really beginning to think more deeply about himself and about Redrock. Unpleasant realities.

He said, 'I've been disturbed by all that's gone on and all I've heard. However, I must do as I said I would do, to Deputy Neal. I gave my word.'

Strickland said, 'I know it. As soon as Jack can manage to make the ride, you'll have to take him in.' Then, 'George, I'm sorry you've got mixed up in this. I sure was a party to that. I'll go along into Redrock an' lay out for Straker what I think.'

'They might not grant you that chance.'

'I can't see any other way to do it. An' Jack's in no shape to go anywhere else, even if you'd allow it.' Strickland could have punched the very air in sheer frustration, cursing the chance that had brought the bountyman, Rudolph Stone, out after Jack. But there was nothing that could be done to change that. What might happen when, eventually, they got back into Redrock, could by no means be predicted. Tom Strickland, however, believing that his brother had been falsely accused, was prepared to defend him to the death.

Halliburton had been speaking very quietly to Jack. Now he straightened up. To Tom, he said, 'Seven, eight more hours, then we'll get mounted. But we'll need to go easy.'

Strickland said, 'We'll need to keep a good look out.' The attack by the masked riders, during which George Halliburton could easily have been hit, had left Strickland with a deep sense of apprehension. Whether those riders had been acting on their own account, seeking the $8,000 reward, or whether they had been sent by others, for other reasons, might never be known. All he hoped was that he had indeed got a hit on one of them, enough to keep them at bay. In an almost bizarre sense the county cage in Redrock looked to be the safest bet for Jack Strickland. There were altogether too many buzzards circling now.

Eleven

Not far into the new day Harry Neal was coming to realize – if he had not done so earlier – that being the sole county lawman was certainly no sinecure. Today, hardly had he set foot in the county office than the newly appointed town marshal came in and on his heels, Jasper Fox. Several more townsmen were outside near the office. Then Mayor Straker, whey-faced and baggy-eyed, put in an appearance.

Fox asked, 'How long yuh gonna wait for Doc Halliburton afore yuh get on out there again?'

Uneasily, Neal said, 'I gotta trust the doc to do what he said he'll do.'

'Yuh'd best hope it comes out right,' Straker said testily. 'There's a known felon out there. Human life's cheap to a man like him. What if they both turn on George Halliburton?'

Neal's uncertainty must have shown. 'Jack Strickland, he's been shot.'

'But Tom Strickland ain't,' Culp said. 'An' we're talkin' here about close kin.'

Neal had no answers. And if he had noticed that, during the course of the posse's return to town, Faulkner and Besant had dropped off, he did not raise that matter.

'Give Halliburton 'til one o'clock,' Straker said. 'If he ain't shown by that time, take another posse out.' Clearly it was an order. They left the office.

Harry Neal himself went out as far as the boardwalk. As well as the general comings and goings of trade, numerous townsmen were standing in small groups. Neal saw that many were armed. It was obvious that the cumulative events of recent days had had a deeply unsettling effect on Redrock. The unknown man who had died under Tom Strickland's pistol had been taken to his last rest, as had the Doyles, father and son. The bountyman, Rudolph Stone, and another whose name apparently had been Al Niebert, together with the attractive woman, Stella Holman, were to be buried today.

Neal's eye, roving Front Street, caught a flicker of garish colour. A couple of whores from the DeLange Hotel. Unusual. Ordinarily they were night people. At any other time he might have been impelled to have a word with them but today had weightier matters on his mind.

On three occasions they had been compelled to halt because Jack Strickland had been in discomfort. Once, Halliburton had unwrapped the gauze bandage and examined the leg wound, pressing gingerly around it, for there were signs of puffy inflammation. An antiseptic salve had been applied but Halliburton feared that there might be an infection.

'The sooner we get to Redrock, the better,'

he said. Then he had a word of warning for Tom Strickland. 'No doubt there'll be a turn-out. Tom, no matter what happens, you can't afford to get into a confrontation.' This was certainly a different Halliburton from the one who had set out.

Though Strickland had travelled warily, half expecting an ambush, nothing transpired, but the constant vigilance had a wearing effect, so it was almost a relief to see, eventually, the rise of the roofs of Redrock, a bluish haze of smoke above it. Yet Tom Strickland had the appalling sense that he was a party to a betrayal.

Coming into the town Strickland became aware not only of the large number of people on Front Street, but that so many of them were armed.

Deputy Harold Neal, swallowing hard and hitching at his belt, stepped down off the boardwalk and came cautiously into the path of the slow-moving horses. And not far off, and approaching, was Brodie Culp wearing his new town marshal's badge; and a soberly dressed Jasper Fox, and Mayor Straker, heading across from his mercantile. The three horsemen had come to a halt. Halliburton lost no time in speaking up.

'Deputy, I'll ask you to stand aside. I have a man who needs special treatment that can't be given out here on the street.'

Neal did take a step to one side but Straker was now right there with Fox and Culp. Flushed with new authority, Culp said, 'Doc, I heard what yuh said to the deputy, but that man yuh brung in, he's got to be put in the county cage. There's an eight-thousand dollar re-ward out fer Jack Strickland. He's a dangerous man.' All eyes were on the gaunt, haggard horseman and the equally unshaven and tired man beside him, the once-county sheriff.

Halliburton raised his voice, 'Stand aside, Mr Culp! This wounded man still happens to be in my care. He'll remain so until he's medically in the clear. Right now I'm about to take him along to my surgery and there he'll stay until I say otherwise.' This firm statement seemed to bring Jasper Fox to slit-mouthed anger.

'You'll not be safe, Doc. None of us will be safe. Yuh can't watch this man day an' night, an' that's what it's gonna take.'

'Nonsense!' It came from Halliburton in what was almost a bark. 'Mr Strickland's wound is in such condition that he wouldn't be capable of getting out on the street, let alone doing anybody in this town a mischief.' He seemed to bite back something more and instead, he repeated his demand to be allowed to move on, unimpeded. Reluctantly, the crowd parted sufficiently to allow Halliburton's horse and Jack Strickland's, to move on, but not before Culp said, 'If he goes to your place, Doc, there's got to be a man posted to see he stays right there.'

Now Jasper Fox said, 'I put up Mr Besant to do it!' Unnoticed, the man named had come easing up behind them. Seeing him there was enough to provoke Tom Strickland to kick his horse forward, causing Fox and several others to step aside in a hurry. 'Where's your sidekick got to, Jake? Where's that asshole Faulkner?'

Besant's expression was nothing short of malevolent. 'Wherever he might be at ain't no ways your concern, Strickland. An' yuh got enough on your plate as it is.'

'Couldn't have put it better,' Culp said. 'There could be charges laid over shelterin' a known felon.'

Halliburton, having had enough of it, said, 'There are other matters that want investigation too. Such as the identity of the two men who attacked our camp after Mr Neal's party had left! Now, make way!' And all three now rode through to the tie rail outside Halliburton's surgery. What Harry Neal had made of Halliburton's angry report of attack was not known, for he said nothing.

Tom Strickland dismounted and moved to help his brother get down. The now silent crowd stood watching as the stiffly moving man, supported by Tom Strickland and the doctor was helped inside the surgery.

Along the street, the undertaker, the tall, angular Lucius Lacey was more intent on catching the eye of Mayor Straker. There were burials to be arranged, and presumably there was the pressing matter of who was to pay. Lacey was much concerned about the three cadavers he now had in open pine boxes in one of his macabre back rooms, after having had to deal with another itinerant in recent times. The county had paid for that one. And for the Doyles. There was another matter on his mind, but Lacey was by nature a most cautious man, certainly not an assertive one. There were some things that were best left unspoken. Perhaps this was one of them. Yet it felt like a small lump of lead in Lacey's stomach.

Besant did not attempt to follow those who had gone inside the surgery but, outside, propped himself against an awning post and began rolling a quirly.

Something unusual was going on at the DeLange Hotel, much to-ing and fro-ing by those who resided there, chattering and whispering together. Anyone who noticed would likely have put it down to feather-brained whores wanting to get a look at the outlaw, Jack Strickland, whose arrival was no doubt seen as something of an event.

Tom Strickland came out of the surgery. He saw Jake Besant propped against the awning post. He said, 'Interfere with what's goin' on in there, an' I promise you'll not straddle your *burro* for a month.'

Besant's lip curled. 'Yuh got no say here no more, Strickland. So yuh kin go clear to Hell an' when yuh git there, tell Ol' Nick I sent yuh.'

Quite deliberately Strickland turned his back and went walking away under the scrutiny of passers-by. Lucius Lacey was no longer to be seen outside his parlour but Strickland found him inside. Lacey's round eyes seemed to enlarge when he saw who his visitor was.

Strickland said, 'I've come to see Stella Holman, an' to pay you.'

With as close as the man would ever get to effusiveness, the undertaker asked, 'For ... uh, all of them?'

Strickland shook his head. 'For the woman. The two hellhounds are somebody else's problem.'

The gangly man made an elaborate play of showing Strickland through to the back room where the coffins were, all three on wooden trestles, lit only by meagre daylight through one small, stained window. Like some hesitant stick insect, Lucius Lacey withdrew.

For some minutes Strickland stood looking at her. Astonishingly Lacey had managed to so place a satin pillow and clean and arrange her thick dark hair that there could be seen little trace of the dreadful head wound. Oddly, she seemed to have shed some years and was more like the old Stella he had known in the past. Whatever her history, whatever dark and unsavoury trails she might have travelled with Jack, or however many times she might have lied for him, she did not deserve to end like this: lying in a cheap box in a smelly little back room in Redrock. The more Strickland looked at her the more did anger seize him. Contemptuously he glanced at Rudolph Stone and the other, said to be a certain Niebert. No more than itinerant scum. Strickland turned and walked out of the room. When he left the parlour, behind him Lacey had momentarily raised one pale hand as though to beckon him back, but in the end did not.

Strickland scarcely noticed street movements or even Jake Besant, but he did take note of Straker, Brodie Culp and Fox coming away from the county office. Maybe they had been in there giving Deputy Neal the hard word about what was to happen to Jack Strickland. Perhaps they now perceived Tom Strickland's demeanour in his purposeful advance, for all three seemed to hesitate. Behind them Harry Neal had come out on the boardwalk as though actually smelling trouble.

Strickland said, 'You'd best hear this now, before you get Jack in front of a judge. Word's come to me that the Doyles probably got it wrong about the four coming out of Torrega, an' it was nothing to do with my brother.'

Recovering from surprise Culp said, 'Two o' that four is long dead. Somewheres up in Nevada.'

Strickland said, 'Dead or not, Jack never moved with Finney or Abbott, that I do know. The Doyles said it was Jack they heard. They got it wrong.'

Culp was already shaking his head. 'Yuh're wastin' your time, Strickland. It's all turned to shit an' there ain't nothin' yuh kin do about it.'

As though he had not even heard, Strickland said, 'What's more, I reckon the Doyles came to think they'd got it wrong. When they got thrown in the cage, somebody thought they might try to buy their way out by tryin' a few other names. That's why they were busted out an' that's why they were shot.'

Fox said, 'All that's pure guesswork. Tryin' to get your kin off the hook, is all.'

It was the reaction that Strickland had expected and he wasn't about to be deflected. 'If they didn't hear *Jack,* then could be what they heard was *Jake.* So why don't you start with Besant an' then find out where his sidekick's got to?'

Harry Neal had drawn closer and was standing a few feet behind Culp and the other two. When he caught Strickland's eye he gave a brief nod. Strickland turned to see Jake Besant approaching slowly, hand already resting on the butt of his pistol.

'Heard my handle mentioned,' he said, 'by this *hombre* here.'

Not sounding as sure as he had earlier, Culp said, 'Take it easy, Jake.'

Strickland had taken a couple of paces out onto Front Street so that he was no longer standing between Besant and the three others. Without taking his eyes off Besant, he said to Culp, 'Go ahead, Brodie, ask him. Ask him about the Torrega bank.' Besant had come to a stop, hand still on the butt of his pistol. When Culp did not ask but, like Fox and Mayor Straker merely stood staring at him, the doubt arising within Besant himself was almost palpable. They were standing there apparently waiting for him to defend himself, to speak out against what Strickland had said. And in that moment, not only must Besant have realized that he was going to have to defend himself, stranded, in this, but Strickland, too, realized it and saw his chance. 'No use to look to these boys for help now, Jake.'

Besant's face had drained of colour and his whole body had tensed. By no means an intelligent man, he was not capable of subtlety or of marshalling a strong argument. All he knew was that suddenly he was under threat here, and those whom he might have expected to spring to his defence were showing not the slightest sign of doing so.

Besant began backing away and Brodie Culp was one of the first to fear what might be about to happen. But instead of calling out some reassurance to Besant in a belated effort to bring him back on side, Culp, in his inexperience, and perhaps in his rather puff-chested view of himself as the new town marshal, also made a cardinal error. Before Strickland or anybody else could warn him against it, Culp made as though to draw his pistol, no doubt, as he saw it, to reinforce his authority in a suddenly dangerous situation. And perhaps with the idea of disarming Besant.

Jake Besant, in Strickland's opinion, was no skilled pistolman, but he sure was better than Brodie Culp. Fox, seeing what was happening, shouted 'No!' but it was too late. Besant pulled his pistol and in a blasting, smoky shot, while the town marshal had not got very far in his draw, hit Culp and spun him half around, Culp crying out, the others, Strickland among them, and Harry Neal, diving to the ground. Still backing off, Besant then turned, in panic, and went running down the nearest alley.

Lucius Lacey, who had been in the act of coming out on the boardwalk, went dodging back inside his sombre place of business. Others on the street, many of them still armed, also made themselves scarce. A show of arms was one thing, facing up to gunfire was quite another.

Twelve

Fox, picking himself up, his neat clothing dusty, suddenly had more to say, calling loudly on Deputy Neal to get about his sworn duty. For the town marshal was shot, Jake Besant gone clear off his head.

'Deputy, this entire town'll stand behind yuh! But it's gotta be done quick!' Strange that such a pronouncement should be made by Fox rather than by Mayor Straker.

Strickland was heading towards Culp who was in considerable distress, down and bleeding and dirty, having rolled in the dusty street. Straker, ashen-faced, seemed transfixed. Somebody else, the frail, ill-looking Fred Earl, was also hastening towards Culp. But it was to Neal that Strickland called.

'Besant's got to be taken alive, Harry!

There's questions to be answered!'

Loudly, Fox said, 'The man's *loco!* Take no risks, Deputy. Shoot Besant if yuh have to!'

Near out of breath, Fred Earl arrived and, without his medical bag at hand, began examining Brodie Culp who was gasping and writhing. Other men were venturing out again. Earl began calling for assistance to move Culp. Some horses at tie rails were restive, backing and tugging at reins.

Belatedly, Mayor Straker shook himself out of his trance. In an unusually reduced voice, he said to nearby townsmen, 'We'll need your help. I ask yuh to do anything the deputy wants.' Nobody seemed enthusiastic. Neal, looking out of his depth did brush by Jasper Fox to make a general statement.

'This here man, Jake Besant, that shot Mr Culp, I gotta find him. There ain't no other deppity.' His eyes flicked to Strickland, then away. 'If'n Jake lights out I'll need a posse. If'n he holes up someplace in Redrock, I cain't go searchin' all over. But anybody helps me, they gotta do like I say an' not commence shootin' weepons off, all over. I reckon Jake's fit to blow the haid off anybody that gits too close.' Neal licked his lips. 'Reckon he'll not come back on Front Street in a hurry. So we all gotta go real easy, checkin' the town.'

By now the groaning Culp had been carried to Earl's rooms. Fox was talking earnestly with Straker. Tom Strickland was moving slowly away. He was still gripped by cold anger after looking at Stella Holman, dead. Culp's downfall had been through the man's own folly. Fox and Straker, watching, wondered no doubt where he might be going. Strickland himself could not have told them. Perhaps to Halliburton's to check on his brother. There had fallen upon the main street of Redrock a most strange hush. The man lately made town marshal had been shot, yet those who might have been expected to go seeking after the culprit seemed almost to be sleepwalking. It would dawn on them soon that, for all that the mayor and some of his committeemen, townsmen and a man of influence, Jasper Fox, and the sole county lawman were unscathed, there was a peculiar lack of leadership, of a will to get things really moving in the search for Jake Besant.

Then with something of an effort, Deputy Neal again raised his voice.

'I need to have men watchin' both ends o' Front Street, an' some more up on roofs. If Jake rides out I wanta know when an' which way.' And with what Strickland thought was surprising forethought, added, 'An' there's a train due in the next hour. I'll have railroad men at the depot watchin' up an' down the track. Folks gittin' off at Redrock, they'll have to wait there at the depot 'til I give 'em the say-so to move anywheres else. Watch out fer any folks headin' fer the depot to git on that train. An' we sure don't want Jake climbin' on it.'

The problem was that Redrock was by no means a small town and it had this hap-hazard, unplanned aspect to it, which meant that there were so many places where a man intent on keeping out of sight, say 'til after sundown, could go to ground and wait. Meantime, any searcher who stumbled on him and raised the alarm could be dead meat in jig-time. The men who would be on the prowl, looking for Besant, showed by their taut faces that they were only too well aware of the hazards. Without doubt, Neal could have wished for a more enthusiastic bunch.

When Strickland looked around he discovered that Jasper Fox had dropped from sight. Straker, however, was now down near Doctor Earl's surgery. On the opposite side of the street from where Straker was, Lucius Lacey had again shown his long face outside his funeral parlour and was now making some hand motions, apparently trying to catch Straker's attention. He was having no success.

Tom Strickland returned to Halliburton's surgery. One of the reasons Straker had failed to notice the attempts by Lacey to attract his attention, was that the Redrock mayor's gaze had for a time been following the progress of the once-county sheriff. Strickland went pacing towards Halliburton's, lighting up a black stogie. Straker was now a man who did not know what to do for the best. The sole remaining deputy seemed far from competent. Certainly he gave no indication of real confidence in spite of his early posting of a few townsmen as lookouts. The fact was that Brodie Culp had been shot and the man who either through panic or stupidity or a bit of both, had done it, had to be arrested, and soon, and thrown in the county cage. Nervously, Straker watched as several of the townsmen, a couple carrying shotguns, others pistols, began moving onto streets branching off Front Street. They were walking slowly and looking as though they would much rather be elsewhere. Straker himself went into the concern that he owned, the mercantile.

Down at the DeLange Hotel there was a lot of nervousness, and for good reason.

Lilah Ford, the woman who ran the place, had returned to one of the upper rooms which for some hours had been declared out of bounds to everyone else. She let herself in.

The man on the brass-framed bed rolled over and grimaced. His shirtless upper body had been generously wrapped around with white gauze bandage. Though clearly still in pain, sweat glistening on face and shoulders, Tex Faulkner had been fortunate to the extent that Tom Strickland's bullet had passed right on through his left side. He had lost a lot of blood and had had to be helped in through the back door of the DeLange by Besant when they had got back to Redrock. Later, two of Lilah's girls had been sent out to a druggist to buy medication and a roll of gauze bandage. And Lilah herself, a woman who was no stranger to the treating of gunshot wounds, had done the doctoring.

Now more than ever Faulkner wanted to know what the hell was going on in Redrock.

189

'That fine friend o' yourn,' Lilah told him, 'he's gone an' shot that greasy li'l bastard Culp.'

Obviously Faulkner was having trouble taking it in. 'What the hell happened? Why'd Jake do that? An' where's Jake at now?'

'Christ, man, how in hell would I know? Lit out, mebbe. But I reckon not, at that. There's fellers wanderin' 'round, all over, lookin'.'

'Fox. Any sign o' Fox?'

'They do say Fox was there at the time. That John Straker an' all.' Lilah sniffed. ''Nother damn' fool. An' that Tom Strickland. It all kinda blew up after him an' Doc Halliburton come in with Jack.'

'Jack Strickland in the cage?'

Lilah shook her head. 'The girls say he's up to Doc Halliburton's own place.'

Faulkner swore in gently shifting his weight. 'Lemme git on my hind laigs... Gimme some help here...'

'Best yuh stay right where yuh are, Tex.'

But she could not persuade him. She

helped him get his feet on the floor. Gasping, he had to wait for close to half a minute before moving across to a window from which he could see across a host of criss-crossing streets to a remote portion of Front Street. Little strings of men were on the move.

On a blind street with no name where, at its end, on three sides were some sun-dried storage buildings separated by overgrown, empty lots, one of the walking townsmen thought he saw movement at one of the blank, glassless windows and gave a shout and then, in panic, fired a smoky shot from the old pistol he was carrying. The two men trailing him went to ground, one holding a pistol, the other a brass-framed 10-gauge shotgun. The man who had fired was backing away, eyes on the window, but there was no answering shot. But on an adjoining street, believing they were being shot at, two other townsmen let fly at nothing in particular, with pistols. There were frantic calls and much confusion.

Straker came to the doorway of the mercantile and was looking up and down Front Street. Lucius Lacey who had been on the point of coming across the street towards the mercantile, at the sound of the shooting changed his mind abruptly and went long-legging back to his own doorway.

Tom Strickland was standing near one of George Halliburton's windows, hoping to see what was happening but, beyond the distant Straker and now the figure of Harry Neal appearing at the mouth of an alley there was nothing to see. Neal was merely looking puzzled.

Behind Strickland, George Halliburton asked, 'Anything?'

Strickland shook his head. 'I might go take a look.'

Now there was the far-off sound of a train whistle. Halliburton, thumbed his watch from a vest pocket. 'On time, today of all days.'

'Harry Neal's just crossed Front Street,' Strickland said. Then, 'For a start I'll take all the horses around back.' He went out and led his own horse, and Jack's and Halliburton's around to a stable in a yard behind the surgery The saddles and other belongings he left in the stables, then took his rifle and Jack's into Halliburton's and propped them in a corner. The sounds of the incoming train were louder now.

Jasper Fox somewhat watchfully walked across Front Street and went inside Doctor Earl's surgery to visit Brodie Culp.

Neal, down a side street, called to some searchers, 'Was that Besant shootin?'

A rooster-necked man in a dirty, collarless shirt and holding a shotgun, shrugged. 'Dunno who it was that shot, Deppity. It warn't in this here street.'

Neal walked on and turned a corner. Yet another dead street lay before him. Neal was on edge. This whole thing was too fragmented. And it was uncanny. Quiet. A few armed men wandering uncertainly about.

From some other street a shot sounded; then another and another. Neal began running. These shots too were heard, all over. There was some shouting. A man ran out on Front Street yelling that a man named Ed Larsen had been shot.

Hearing it, Straker shouted to those behind him in the mercantile, 'Besant's shot Ed Larsen!'

But the man who had come running was shaking his head. 'It warn't Jake Besant. Luke Ambrose, he thought Ed was Besant an' took a fly shot an' hit Ed!'

Harry Neal was arriving at that particular scene. Larson's left sleeve was covered in blood and he was holding that arm with his other hand. Two other men were with him, and another, looking whey-faced and shaken, was arriving. He was carrying an old Henry rifle.

'Jesus! I took 'im fer Besant. Same colour shirt an' all!'

Harry Neal told him to shut his mouth. 'Jes' git Ed took to a doc!'

Jasper Fox was now back at Culp's saloon. Even he was looking on edge, not knowing what was happening. By this time Straker had left the mercantile and gone across to Halliburton's surgery, not to see the doctor but looking for Tom Strickland. On his way over, some men had appeared further up Front Street, helping another across towards Doc Earl's. They called out to the mayor, letting him know what was going on, and that Ed was shot in the arm.

About that same time the train could be heard, now chuffing out of Redrock. No doubt apprised of what was taking place in Redrock, the crew would be only too pleased to be on their way.

Tom Strickland was still talking with Dr Halliburton. They turned to look at the Redrock mayor when he came scuttling in. Straker hardly paused to draw breath.

'Tom, we gotta talk!'

Strickland said, 'We finished all our talking when I turned in the badge. You here to tell me I'll face charges over sheltering a felon?'

Straker, his small eyes shuttling between

Strickland and Halliburton, said, 'There's been a man shot. Not by that dam' hare-brained Besant, but by another of 'em that's out there around the streets.'

'Then you'd best advise the deputy to call 'em all back in,' Halliburton snapped. 'In something like this, the ordinary man is way out his depth. I never thought to see the day when I would be attacked, have bullets fired at me. It's an experience I never want to go through again.'

'That's ... what I've come about. This ... situation. Tom, Deputy Neal can't do this on his own. An' he can't do it with a bunch of jumpy townsmen. If ever this county needed ... a professional, it needs one now.' Just getting the words out must have cost Straker.

Strickland said, 'It's not as simple as that. I'm concerned only for my brother, in there.'

Halliburton jumped in again. 'And I can tell you I've come to the view that Jack Strickland was nowhere near that Torrega bank. You might say it can't be proved; the man does not have to prove it. Only others who were involved at Torrega could possibly say. Locating Mr Besant could well clear that up. You know as well as I do that it was what triggered this latest outrage.'

Straker stood blinking at the doctor. He knew he must take heed of a statement as plain as that from a respected physician. Then Strickland asked, because it was still troubling him, 'Where's Tex Faulkner got to?'

Straker shook his head. 'I don't know...'

'Then maybe he's dead,' said Strickland. 'If I did hit one of them, at the camp, he could be. Or hurt, somewhere. Why don't you go ask Fox some hard questions?'

Straker's face coloured. 'Mr Fox is a man who's got a lot of money invested in this place. In this county.'

'An' looking to invest some more,' Strickland said harshly. 'But it's not near enough for the farmers up along the northern Slee. Last time Fox went out there to talk with 'em, he took Jake Besant along. Did you know that?'

Straker started to say, 'I know nothing of–'

'Then you go ask Fox.' Yet Strickland knew it was unlikely that Straker would do so.

Halliburton had been studying Strickland. 'Tom, it's not up to me to tell you what you ought to do. But it's plain that there'll be no safety here until this affair is resolved, one way or another. My fear is that others are going to get hurt before it's finished.'

Strickland sighed and nodded. 'I'll go see if I can locate Harry Neal.' Without a glance at the Redrock mayor, he left.

When, a minute or so later, Straker came out, Strickland was nowhere to be seen. But Lucius Lacey was. He was making more of his urgent hand movements. Straker went along to find out what the hell the undertaker could possibly want at a time like this.

Strickland, having immediately left Front Street, now encountered two men, one apparently unarmed, the other with a

Remington pistol. Both shrugged when he asked, 'Where's Harry Neal?'

They had seen the deputy about ten minutes ago but only briefly. Strickland walked on. Soon he clambered over the poles of an empty corral and came to a small, rutted area bordered on three sides by ramshackle structures and a pile of lumber, sun-curled and with weeds growing through it. From there he made his way to a backstreet where he saw Neal talking with some townsmen. When he reached them, Neal asked, 'You in this now, Tom?'

'Could be. But not wearing a badge. You're the man in charge. You want my advice, ask for it.'

The first thing Neal did was advise the townsmen to get on home. They left, their relief scarcely concealed. When they were out of earshot, Neal said, 'I hear some folks come off the train. The railroad boys are holdin' 'em at the depot. Wherever Jake's got to his ass is likely afire because no bastard talked up fer him. Tex Faulkner's dropped out o' sight. There's still on'y one man Jake could turn to, an' that's Fox. Even after what happened. He cain't lie low forever, Tom, but if he does, 'til after sundown, we got a real problem.'

Strickland asked, 'Where's Jake's horse?'

'Dunno that. Could be in some barn somewheres.' It was simply that there were too many places to look. And maybe there were people around still who would be inclined to keep their mouths shut.

Looking about them carefully, Strickland and Deputy Neal walked towards Front Street, but before they got that far, Strickland said, 'You go on. I'm gonna take a look across there.' A short string of clapboard dwellings stood just a little way beyond what once had been a small corral. Few of its twisted poles remained. Picking his way through, Strickland went past one house, then another. At the fourth, near a window, he glimpsed a woman's face. He passed on by, walking unhurriedly. Sixty or seventy feet on, he entered an overgrown, empty lot. He had to avoid random bits of junk that had been dumped there. Satisfied that the place could not be overseen by the house where he had noticed the woman, for another dwelling now stood in between, he paused.

He was quite sure that he had detected fear in the woman's face. He believed that he had found Jake Besant.

What Strickland decided to do would no doubt bring Neal and probably others at the run but he had to gamble that it would also cause Jake Besant to get careless, maybe bring him out of hiding, to look.

For Besant was indeed inside that house, pistol drawn and almost touching the head of a boy of about fourteen years old. On the sly move, Besant had thought he had heard searchers almost on top of him and had sought cover in the nearest of the houses in the vicinity.

The woman was still standing near the window. Besant, big, powerful, his unshaven face sweatslick, asked, 'They gone?'

'He's gone.' Trying to control her voice,

she said, 'There was but one. Tall, stoopy man, him that was the county sheriff.'

Plainly Besant had not expected this. Damn Fox to hell. And Brodie Culp. When accusations had been made they had both stood there, dumb, not talking up for him. The rage that had seen him draw on the fool Culp had not abated. But if he could keep out of sight 'til sundown he would get on out of Redrock. There was no way that Faulkner would be in any shape to ride with him but that couldn't be helped. Then the sounds came.

Tom Strickland, down on one knee, had wadded his red bandanna and pushed it firmly into the soft, grassy earth. He pressed the muzzle of the pistol against the wad and fired. Then a second time. The sounds were oddly muffled but would still carry. He then made his way across to the corner of the house that stood nearest to him and stood waiting, watching the yard door of its neighbour.

For a short time it seemed that his ruse

would not work, that Besant's curiosity would not get the better of him. Then suddenly there he was, out on the porch, pistol in hand, big head lifted slightly as though sniffling the breeze, trying to work out the direction the shooting had come from. By his reckoning a little distance off, it could well draw the deputy and give him, Besant, the chance to slip away. Yet to do so he would have to reach his horse which, right now, along with Faulkner's mount, was in a stable close to the back of the DeLange Hotel.

Tom Strickland, pistol in hand, stepped into view.

'Throw it down, Jake. Don't do anything harebrained.'

Behind Besant the yard door was slammed shut and bolts were shot home. She had been waiting for her chance. Besant's pistol was coming up but he must have known he was not going to get it done in time, not up against Strickland.

Then from an upper window of the De-

Lange Hotel, two blocks away, Faulkner's rifle lashed and the bullet kicked into Strickland's left arm, blood flying, and pitched him bodily against the corner of the house, and down he went. Besant took his chance and bolted. Yet he did not head for the DeLange Hotel. Even a dullard such as Besant had concluded that the rifle shot from that place would fetch Deputy Neal at a gallop.

Harry Neal was in fact with Straker at the mercantile, holding in his hand a flimsy scrap of paper that the Redrock mayor had given to him, he having had it from Lucius Lacey. Then the distant-sounding pistol shots had gone off and not long after them, the lashing report of a rifle. Neal began running in the direction of the shooting, drawing his pistol as he went. Passing Culp's saloon he glimpsed Jasper Fox, but resisted the impulse to check his stride and speak with that man. But he did call to him.

'Stay right in there, mister! I'll be back!' If Harry Neal surprised himself, he certainly surprised Fox, a man unaccustomed to being spoken to in that manner and more especially by a young county deputy who, indeed, Fox had no high regard for. Neal went jogging on. When he came to the street on which he had last seen Tom Strickland, he found the man again, coming unsteadily away from one of the houses there, his left sleeve darkly stained, blood dripping from the ends of his fingers.

Between teeth that were clenched, Strickland said, 'Besant's on the move. But I got this from a rifle an' I'd say it was upstairs, at the DeLange. Faulkner would be my guess.'

'Where's Jake headed?'

'The other way, yonder. Been holed up in one of these houses.' Strickland was in pain but he said, 'Get after Faulkner. Get that goddamn' rifle off him.'

Neal began moving away but paused in going and gave Strickland the scrap of paper handed to him by Straker. 'Lacey, he found it on Niebert.' And he added, 'I'll deal with that, later.' He left, heading for the DeLange. Strickland, though not moving well, had made up his mind that, as best he might, he would follow Jake Besant. His left arm was hanging limply.

Sweating, breathing deeply, Strickland began picking his way through the back lots, among the storehouses of Redrock. At every shambling step he expected to be confronted by the man he was seeking and was only too well aware that he would now be at a grave disadvantage. Yet now that he had once sighted the man, he felt that, until Harry Neal could deal with the situation at the DeLange, he must try to keep Besant on the move while some daylight yet remained.

At the DeLange, Neal was allowing no one to impede his progress. Partly clad women got out of the way as the deputy, long pistol in his hand, went bounding up the main staircase. Lilah Ford would have hindered him though.

'Faulkner! Which goddamn' room, Lilah?' When she began shaking her head he promised he would hammer lead through every door he came to. 'Then, when I've got the bastard, I'll shut this shit-hole down an' put you an' every other whore on the next train out!'

Lilah Ford had never seen Harry Neal as worked up as he was now, and an involuntary turn of her head told him what he was demanding to know. Neal positioned himself just to one side of the door and with a racketing, smoky shot blew the lock apart. To one swinging boot the flimsy door swung quiveringly open. Neal was still standing off to one side when Faulkner's rifle went off, blowing a dusty hole in the plaster wall of the passageway. Without exposing all of his body, swiftly Neal fired into the room twice. Faulkner's rifle went clattering to the floor. Neal sprang to the open doorway and blasted again and Faulkner, already hit, was hit again and went bumping against the frame of the open window. Coming forward into the room, Neal shot him again and this time Faulkner doubled over and, half turning, fell out, uttering not one sound.

Smoking pistol hanging at his side, Neal walked downstairs. In the dirty alley alongside the hotel, he found Tex Faulkner, dead. As he walked away, Neal began reloading the pistol, his face a mask of fury.

Tom Strickland had by now reached an area of Redrock that was a jumble of buildings of all kinds, and some corrals. Across to his left, however, stood the backs of taller buildings facing Front Street, among them the one where George Halliburton's surgery was. Something made Strickland turn. Fifty feet away, having emerged from behind him, was Jake Besant, and he was in the act of lining up a pistol.

Strickland took a desperate gamble, staggering to one side and firing his own pistol, a snap shot, let fly without much hope of hitting his man. But, as he had hoped, the quick action was just enough to cause Besant to flinch and to fire too quickly. Lead went breathing past Strickland's head. But now he stumbled and fell and the pistol dropped from his grasp. His left arm was afire with pain, and momentarily his vision blurred. Besant, arm extended, lined him up again, this time making sure.

A shot lashed out and suddenly Besant was hit hard, back-stepping, and was hit again, this loud shooting coming from more or less behind Strickland. Besant fell on his back and was making only small twitching movements, no more than spasms. When Strickland turned his head to look, it was to see his brother shoulder-propped in Halliburton's yard doorway, in the act of levering another round into the chamber of a Winchester, the ejected shell brassily glinting in its parabola. Halliburton's anxious face could just be discerned over Jack Strickland's shoulder.

Very slowly, Strickland got to his feet. He made his way across to Halliburton's yard door. At once the doctor wanted to treat Strickland's ravaged arm. Strickland, however, groped around and produced the flimsy piece of paper that Harry Neal had given him. Halliburton read the message aloud. It was a telegram sent by Jasper Fox to a man named Al Niebert, to bring that man to Redrock.

'Lucius Lacey found it on Niebert's body. Lacey showed it to Straker. Straker gave it to Harry.'

They had heard muffled gunfire from the other end of Redrock.

Halliburton asked, 'Where's Neal now?'

'He went to the DeLange. Faulkner's there.' Strickland glanced at his useless left arm. 'As well I know.'

Even as Strickland said it they saw Neal approaching across the back lots. A different Harry Neal. Slit-mouthed. Bleak. Worn. Older.

Halliburton was aghast. 'Jasper Fox!' He was having trouble equating what he had read for himself, with a man who had been regarded as one of the county's leading lights.

Jack Strickland said, 'This Fox, from what

Tom's said, he was among them that was quick to shit on my name after the Doyles come in with their tale.'

Tom said, 'Neither Besant nor Faulkner have ever been far away from where Fox was at any time. I'd guess he knew, or had a damn' good idea, that they were among the four at the Torrega bank. Maybe he was holding that over 'em. Then, when I put the Doyles in the cage, it was safer to bust 'em out an' shut their mouths for good an' all, rather than have 'em buy their way out with a changed story that let Jack off the hook an' maybe put the other two on it. Jase Lowell maybe got onto something, asked some questions. Enough to rattle 'em. Guess-work, of course. But now we do know it must've been Fox that set Niebert on Jack.'

'And could have killed any or all of us,' Halliburton said.

In a curiously tight voice, Neal said, 'I've already given Fox the word I want to talk with him.'

Strickland thought it might not have been

the wisest thing to have done. He said, 'Hard to say what Fox might do now. Culp's out of it, that's one thing. So is Besant, an' Fox, he'll likely soon hear of it.'

'An' so is Tex Faulkner out of it,' Neal said. 'He's dead, in the alley down by the DeLange.'

Jack Strickland said, 'For all we know, there could be others in Fox's pocket. I'd take it slow an' easy, Deputy. Where's he at?'

'Last I seen he was at Culp's.'

'Then that's where we'll go,' Strickland said.

'You can't do it,' Halliburton said. 'Not with the way that arm looks to be.'

'I want to see this through,' Strickland said. 'Fox, to my way of thinking, is one of the *hombres* that brought it all down on us. I want to be there at the finish.' And he would not be dissuaded.

Fox was no longer in sight at the Cattlemen's. Neal asked some sharp questions there but got no help at all. It was apparent that there were still men in that place who were willing – or cautious enough – to give nothing away.

Neal, with the bloodied and dishevelled Tom Strickland, walked out, Strickland somewhat unsteadily, but he said to Neal, 'Let's go take a look around back.'

When they got there it was to discover Fox in the act of entering a barn in which a couple of horses could be seen.

'Told yuh I'd be back,' Neal said, 'an' I told yuh to stay where yuh was.'

'So yuh did, Deputy,' Fox said, unruffled, 'but it so happens I've got some business to attend to, out of Redrock.'

'Up on the northern Slee?' Strickland asked.

Fox's eyes flicked to the man with the badly bloodied arm. 'My business, Strickland, is just that. My business.'

'Ain't yuh gonna en-quire where your boys is at?' Neal asked. 'Anyways, I've brung news about 'em. One daid in an alley, attractin' flies. T'other jes' as daid up in back o' Halliburton's. When it come to the point, neither of 'em was much good.'

If he had not known this already, Fox took it without visible evidence of surprise. He shrugged and would have turned away had not Strickland, who was having some trouble seeing clearly, said, 'Now all that's left to talk about is the telegram you sent to Al Niebert.'

Standing quite still, Fox stared at him.

Neal said, 'So we got to git on down to the county office, Mr Fox, an' we got to have us a heart-to-heart about a few things.'

Fox must have seen that Neal was not about to be argued with. He said, 'Sure thing, Deputy, I'll come on down there.' He slipped a button and held his well-cut jacket partly open. 'As yuh can see, I'm carryin' no weapon, so yuh've got no problems.'

Neal nodded, turning away. 'Then the sooner we gits it done, the better.'

Strickland had to blink to be certain that what he then thought he saw was actually happening, Fox's hand first sliding inside his jacket and coming out again holding a derringer. Strickland yelled, 'Harry-?

From some deep reserve Strickland summoned strength and speed and drew his pistol and as the long barrel came up, he blasted a smoky shot away even as the derringer cracked like a snapping twig. But Fox's shot had been driven wide by the impact of Strickland's .44 lead punching him in the chest and dumping him down on the hardpack. Strickland went staggering forward and kicked the fallen derringer away. Fox's eyes dilated, then went opaque, and one hand that he had partly raised, fell limply back.

Neal, having turned belatedly, swallowed hard then stepped across quickly to steady Strickland. He said, 'Turnin' my back on that bastard is the last damn' fool thing I'll ever do, Tom.'

'Tell that to Straker. An' his guild. An' tell it to the county when they call another election for sheriff.'

Men were coming out from a back door of the saloon. Neal said, 'Leave this here feller right where he's at. By an' by, Lucius Lacey, he'll come git him when he's cleanin' up all the other garbage.'

Leaning on Harry Neal, Strickland allowed himself to be led out of the yard and away along Front Street, back towards Halliburton's.

Thirteen

The shock over all that had happened was not about to lift easily from Redrock. The strange hush that had fallen all across the town persisted with the dying of the light. Indeed it was some little time before many folk in the town could allow themselves to be assured that all gunfire was truly over.

Faces at many of the windows had looked on as Lucius Lacey had gone about the macabre business of removing the bodies of the dead. Indeed, Lacey's dingy rooms were filling up with cadavers, and the undertaker had already, and again, taken his concerns about payment to Mayor Straker. To what outcome, no one else knew.

Strickland, his left arm in a black sling, had noticed Lacey going inside the mercantile and had permitted himself an icy smile, guessing what the visit would be about. Jack Strickland was still at Halliburton's, while Deputy Harry Neal had gone back to his unappealing rooming-house and his bed, the county office securely locked behind him.

The passengers who had arrived on the afternoon train had been released from the waiting-room at the depot, and Strickland, having been given a personal message, was now heading for the Salinger House Hotel. As he walked along Front Street several townsfolk had made as though to speak to him, but his demeanour had been such that all had thought better of it, merely staring at his back after he had passed by.

At the Salinger House they would have had him cool his heels in the lobby but, already aware of the room number he wanted, he had taken no notice and gone right up. To his brief knock and his word, the occupant in 27 had opened the door.

She looked as good as ever he could recall, small, neat, her fair hair coiled thickly,

218

shinily behind her ears. There was but brief contact, a mere half embrace before she stepped back and studied him, his dishevelled clothing, his black arm sling.

'This is real strange, Tom. Coming back to this. To what's been happening here. It was this, all this that drove me to go away in the first place.'

'I'd not reckoned to see you again, Grace.'

'I'd not thought to be here, either.'

'Why, then?'

There was a small movement of her straight, narrow shoulders, as close to a shrug as she would ever come. 'I've had plenty of time to think. On my own.'

He drew a long breath. 'So. What now?'

After a few seconds she said, 'Nothing. Not too soon. Take things a day at a time.'

'You'll stay here at the Salinger?'

'Yes, for the time being.' Then, 'Can you understand that?'

'Yeah, I reckon so.'

Presently she said, 'This whole place is alive with talk. About you. About Jack.'

'Jack was hurt. Shot. But he's near to back on his feet. He's down at George Halliburton's.' There were things, however, that Grace Strickland had not yet heard, and her slightly raised eyebrows were asking the next question. He said, 'Stella's dead.'

'*Dead?*' Her long, slim fingers went to her lips.

'At a camp, where Jack was. A bountyman, Al Niebert. It's a long story.' He looked down. She did not ask *How do you feel about that, Tom?* If she had he would not have known how to answer, for he did not know, for sure, himself. During past hours his molten anger had buried any deeper feelings he might have had.

She said, 'You look dead on your feet. You'd best go get some rest.' Then, 'Thank you, for coming.'

Wearily, he nodded. 'I'll come by again in the morning. We can talk.' At the door he paused as though to say something more, but in the end did not, and went out, quietly closing the door behind him.

She was back. There might yet be some way to go, rebuilding, but it was something. A beginning. Seventy yards away, at Lacey's, Stella Holman lay in waxen death. Yet maybe the past few minutes, in Room 27 at the Salinger House, presaged a new start of life.

The publishers hope that this book has given you enjoyable reading. Large Print Books are especially designed to be as easy to see and hold as possible. If you wish a complete list of our books please ask at your local library or write directly to:

Dales Large Print Books
Magna House, Long Preston,
Skipton, North Yorkshire.
BD23 4ND

This Large Print Book for the partially sighted, who cannot read normal print, is published under the auspices of
THE ULVERSCROFT FOUNDATION